INTO CHAOS

Edited by Sam Agar,
Paula Dias Garcia
and Marc Clohessy

LIMERICK, 2022

INTO CHAOS
ISBN: 978 1 7391383 1 8
PUBLISHED BY Sans. PRESS
December 2022
Limerick, Republic of Ireland

COVER ARTWORK & ILLUSTRATIONS by Dominique Ramsey
LAYOUT & BOOK DESIGN by Paula Dias Garcia
TYPESET in Arno Pro and Bicyclette

EDITORS
Sam Agar, Paula Dias Garcia and Marc Clohessy

www.sanspress.com
 @PressSans
 sans.press
 /sans.press

INTO CHAOS receives financial assistance
from the Arts Council.

EDITOR'S NOTE

Paula Dias Garcia

Coming up on our fourth anthology, it has become a game for our team to try and guess what stories this round of submissions will bring. Since we'd asked for stories where characters take a step beyond all they've known and embrace chaos, that's where our minds were. Parallel dimensions, intergalactic travel and alien civilisations! Magic portals! Mayhem and destruction and surely, *surely*, the end of the world.

As always, we got *some* of it right, but missed the big surprise. Don't worry – you can be assured going in that every story in this collection delivers chaos in its own particular way. Sometimes it's magic, sometimes it's science, and on occasion it's mere reality, devastatingly refusing to bend to what one needs or desires.

But if they're different in the ways they explore chaos, every story in this anthology has surprised us by showing at its core a relentless quest for joy and beauty.

Through dangerous journeys, beauty shines through; hearts beset by grief find space for more love; the portals are crossed in undying hope. And yes, sometimes it *is* the end of the world, and yet joy manages to shine through. Be it in hopes of the future or in memories of the past, it is always present, undeniable – and shining through the connections formed.

We expected the chaos part, of course, but there was something remarkable in the way that it was *embraced*, with a steadfast refusal to give up the very best of life.

So, once again, we're surprised, and incredibly grateful. To everyone that has believed in our project and our calls, the booksellers, the Arts Council, and every single writer that has put their own spin on what it means to step into chaos.

We can't wait to see how you'll surprise us again!

THE STORIES

CONTENT WARNINGS

What the Water Left Behind: drowning (referenced);
   death of a parent (mentioned), societal collapse; aftermath
   of natural disaster.

Sweethope Fair: missing children; dementia (implied);
   sexual content.

American Short Fiction, 1800-1999: societal collapse; self-harm;
   suicidal ideation (implied); mental decline; murder (implied).

As Light, Unraveling: suicidal ideation (implied).

While I'm Still Here: abduction; murder; mild gore.

To All Those Who Exist In The Universe: gun violence;
   societal collapse (implied).

You'll Be Gone by Morning: death of loved ones; death of
   an infant (mentioned); injury detail.

Penelope: sexual content.

Connections Carved in Starlight: body modification;
   mild eye gore; sexual content.

Fellow in the Firmament: mental distress.

Aisling: violence; substance abuse; sexual abuse (implied).

Tank: dysphoria; self-harm ideation.

"Though my soul may set in darkness,
it will rise in perfect light;
I have loved the stars too fondly
to be fearful of the night."

SARAH WILLIAMS,

The Old Astronomer

WHAT THE WATER LEFT BEHIND

Jennifer Hudak

When the water receded, crabs scuttled sideways across the lower rooftops, snapping crescent claws. Seaweed draped the buildings and lampposts in glistening finery. As for the sidewalks and streets, they were strewn with shells: Fibonacci-whorled, flat and ridged, cupped like spoons. The children snatched the best ones and plunged them into pockets, where they jingled alongside useless coins and sodden sweet wrappers and transit cards.

Kora, though hardly more than a child herself, barely glanced at the shells crunching beneath her feet. Once – back when she still lived with her father instead of her street family – she prized the mussel shells. The tiny ones reminded her of sculpted fingernails, and their dull grey exteriors reminded her that beauty – gleaming and pearlescent – could be hidden anywhere. But she had no time now to gather shells. Now, she kept her eyes forward instead of down.

At the end of the block, the entrance to the subway yawned open. The wooden barriers had already been pushed aside, the tape torn away. That meant the rescue workers had come and gone, the bodies had been cleared, and the tunnels belonged to the fishers. It took the city days to dry out after each storm, but the subways never drained, not completely. The water down here – oily, opaque – was toxic. Kora knew this. But, like everything, fishing was a calculated risk. The subway was where the water carried everything it stole. Most people were too afraid to fish – afraid of the dark, of the water, of the corpses they might find floating in the canals. Kora couldn't blame them. She was afraid of those things, too. But unlike some of the others, she didn't have a choice. And as long as people like her were willing to take the risk, those above-ground would trade well for what she found.

At the bottom of the stairs, the water was already knee-deep. Kora waded toward a dark, flooded supply room. Ignoring the weight of the water in her shoes, she uncovered the plastic shipping container she'd been using as a boat. The pole she normally used for steering leaned against the wall next to the container, but today, Kora left it where it was. Instead, she chose a new pole, one left behind by a long-absent fisher. This pole had a cruel hook affixed to one end, and Kora handled it carefully. It was the pole of a lobster – a bottom-feeder who scraped the tracks for bigger hauls.

Kora had always taken care to give the lobsters a wide berth, especially those who were leaning over the side of their boats, straining to pull up something heavy. Lobstering was dangerous. Sooner or later, all lobsters capsized and wound up at the bottom themselves, and if you got too close, you might get dragged down with them. Kora had always focused her fishing on whatever had floated to the surface: cups, plastic bottles and containers, sometimes even those waterproof foam shoes. None of it was as valuable as what might have sunk to the bottom, but it was safer.

Lately, though, Kora hadn't had much luck with her fishing. Perhaps people were learning how to keep their possessions safe from the relentless storms; perhaps the police and rescue crews had gotten wise and started fishing for more than bodies. Whatever the reason, the waters were emptier after each flood, Kora's catches less valuable. The best night market vendors, the ones who used to happily trade her slivers of fermented fish and swigs of crab-apple wine, now averted their eyes when she approached their tables. Her street family had been kind, offering her a bit of food and a dry place to sleep even when Kora couldn't contribute to their stores, but their charity wouldn't last forever.

She turned the new pole in her hands. It felt strange in her grip – oddly-balanced, heavier than she was used to. She wondered who'd made it, and if they'd died, or just retired. She wondered what it said about her that she didn't much care either way.

Kora tamped down the panic rising in her chest, and carried both the hooked pole and the shipping container to the canal covering the subway tracks. The current today was strong. She'd barely hopped into the container before it drifted into the dark tunnel, heading downtown. Once the curving subway walls hemmed her in, the tinny echo of the water lapping against the sides of the tunnel made Kora feel like she was the only person left alive. When she passed a lobster, their raft anchored to the bottom, it was something of a relief, and Kora waved.

The lobster just growled at her. 'You better not be thinking of setting up here. This is my area.'

'What? I mean, I wasn't stopping. I was just passing by.'

The lobster thrust his chin at her hook. 'Bet you don't even know how to use that thing, do you?' He sniffed, and then turned back to his own pole. 'Doesn't matter. We're all just fighting for scraps down here. You'll see.'

By the time he finished talking, Kora had drifted far enough that she'd have to shout at him if she wanted to reply, so she stayed silent. Before long, he was just another shadow in the darkness, and it was slightly easier to pretend to ignore what he'd said.

After floating with the current for a bit longer, Kora opened the salvaged plastic bag she kept tied to her belt loop and pulled out an empty milk jug and a length of nylon rope. With cold, shaking fingers, she tied one end of the rope to the handle of the jug. Then she paused. There were no holes in her container, no rings set into it that she could tie the rope to. She had no idea how the lobsters stayed anchored; she'd never gotten close enough to ask one.

After a moment's thought, she tied the other end of the rope to her ankle. Then, carefully, she dipped the jug into the canal. She felt the weight of it in her hands, felt the pull of the water. But before it tipped the boat, she let the bottle go. It settled down at the bottom of the canal. Her boat drifted another foot or two until the rope grew taut, tugging at her ankle and holding her in place.

The rope dug into her skin as the current pulled against it, and panic squeezed her heart like an actual fist. When she first started fishing, she'd suffered these moments of panic every time she entered the subway – when the darkness of the tunnel swallowed up the daylight, when the chill from the water bit at her skin, when the smell hit her like a physical presence. The only way she could get through them was by remembering the nights she'd spent stargazing with her father. This was back when he was alive, back when the storms had just started, when the ocean had only just begun to encroach on the city. On clear nights, he'd teach her how to recognise the North Star, brilliant as a diamond. He hadn't known the names of the others, so together, he and Kora had invented new constellations – the Firefly, the Bat, the Snail, the Dinosaur – and made up their own mythologies.

It had been ages since she'd needed the comfort of those stories to make it through the water, but today – heart pounding, ears ringing – she tried again. 'Once upon a time, Firefly decided to go into the deepest, darkest forest,' she whispered to herself. 'The creatures of the forest laughed at Firefly, for she had no weapon, only her light.'

But the story didn't touch the fear lodged in Kora's chest. She'd been doing this too long; she knew too much. There was no magic down here in the subway. There was no light at all. There was only the water, and the things the water carried away.

She awkwardly lifted the blunt end of her pole out of the water and turned it over, putting it back in the canal hook-side-down. Then, she began to drag the hook across the bottom in wide arcs. It skipped over the tracks and stirred up sludge. The lobster was right; she didn't know how to use this pole. She didn't know what she was doing at all.

But then, surprisingly quickly, the hook snagged on something. She gave an experimental tug; whatever she'd caught was soft and heavy: a blanket, perhaps, or a coat. Kora flushed with excitement, imagining the price she'd get for such an item at the night market. Or maybe, maybe she'd dry it out and keep it to wrap around herself when the cold winds came. Either way, it was a prize. She gripped the pole and braced it against the side of her container, trying to lift up whatever she'd caught, but it wouldn't budge. She raised herself up to half-kneeling, and tried again.

The hook, suddenly freed, whipped up out of the water. Kora fell back onto her seat and, for a horrible moment, thought she'd capsize. Water sloshed into the container, soaking her up to her waist. After a sickening couple of rocks back and forth, the container stabilised and resumed bobbing in the centre of the canal. With her heart still pounding in her ears, Kora pulled in the pole to get a better look at what she'd caught.

Seaweed. That's all it was. Long and lanky and most likely toxic, it had been tangled in the tracks before her hook had ripped it free.

For a long moment Kora sat, shivering with the cold and the damp. When she finally worked up the courage to plunge the hook back into the water, the container wobbled back and forth, and her stomach seized. The tug of the rope against her ankle felt like someone reaching out of the canal, trying to pull her overboard.

'Firefly's light revealed eyes peering out from the darkness,' she whispered while she dragged the pole along the bottom, 'and the gleam of teeth.' Her voice trembled and hitched with her breath. That couldn't be how the story went. She tried to imagine her father's voice, his finger tracing patterns in the sky, but the memory had long ago lost focus. Would she even remember the constellations if she saw them? How long had it been since she'd looked at the sky?

Kora's hands ached and she stretched out her fingers. She'd been scraping the tracks for what felt like hours, and had nothing to show for it but soaking wet pants.

We're all just fighting for scraps here, the lobster had said. Was this what he meant? Was the canal finally picked clean of everything but takeout containers and seaweed?

Maybe she just needed to pull up her anchor and find another spot. She balanced the pole crosswise on the container and untied the rope from her ankle. The container immediately started drifting again, and before Kora knew what was happening, the end of the rope slipped out of her cold fingers and into the canal like a water snake. Within seconds, it was gone.

'No…!' Her voice, bouncing against the tunnel walls, sounded hollow and false. Kora watched her lobstering spot drift further and further away with an odd sense of detachment. She'd lost her plastic jug – and her rope – but did it really matter? She didn't know how to lobster. She wasn't going to catch anything no matter where she anchored.

Kora knew she should start poling herself back upstream; the further she went, the longer the journey back would take. But she'd caught nothing today that she could trade. There was no reason to go to the night market at all. When the current carried her further downstream, into the no man's land between stations, Kora let it.

The tunnel darkened the further she went. Sometimes, a red-tinged emergency light flickered overhead, but most of the bulbs were dead. Kora widened her eyes against the darkness and tried to keep from shivering. She had heard stories about fishers who'd drifted too far and gotten lost among the branching tunnels, or who'd gotten washed out to sea. Either way, they never saw daylight again.

But she was so tired. Her arms ached from fighting the current day after day. Nothing ever changed. The storms would keep coming. The subways would never drain. All paths led to the bottom of the water; some just led there more quickly than others.

When she saw the lights shining on the tracks down below, she thought that it was just the beginning of a migraine – a flicker of an aura in the corners of her eyes. But the lights were steady, even when she looked at them directly. Centring herself carefully in her makeshift boat, she peered into the depths.

Pinpricks of bioluminescence drew the outlines of dozens of sea creatures. Small, slightly bulbous, tentacled, they fed on the scum and algae that covered the sides and bottom of the canal, and lit the water with their soft, otherworldly glow. She wondered how long they'd been here. She wondered if they'd been washed into the tunnels by the storms like everything else – or if they'd chosen this new ecosystem. If, like her, they'd had to adapt to evolving circumstances. Kora stared at them, forgetting the damp, forgetting the cold. They looked so fragile, with their delicate fronds and their gentle lights, as if they might tear like tissue in the strong current. And yet they didn't. They were here, and whole: darting to and fro in their curious work, as oblivious to Kora as she'd previously been to them.

Kora didn't quite know why she was so transfixed by the lights beneath the water. Nothing had changed. She hadn't caught anything today, and she'd go to her street family nearly empty-handed once again. She'd come back to fish in this depleted canal tomorrow, and the day after that, poling herself through the water until she lost the strength to return aboveground. The existence of the sea creatures shouldn't *matter* to her, not really. Still, she couldn't stop her eyes from pricking with tears. Because even as the storms raged and the ocean roiled, even as the trains floated out to sea and the fishers scavenged the subways until nothing of value was left – even then, sea creatures could thrive in poisoned water, as hidden and as beautiful as the interior of a mussel shell.

'The forest was dark and bristling with claws and teeth and spines,' Kora whispered, 'but Firefly's light found magic in it all the same.' That wasn't the actual ending of the story. It was just the middle; there was more to it, and Kora couldn't remember if Firefly made it out of the forest in the end. But right now, it didn't matter. Right now, the magic was enough. Kora skimmed a fingertip over the water, tracing submerged constellations, and felt something deep in her chest unclench.

Kora emerged from the subway tunnel to find the sun setting behind the buildings, drenching the sky in pinks and oranges. In the dusk, the lights of the night market shone in the distance; the breeze carried a delicious, fishy scent. Kora's stomach rumbled, but she ignored it. She crumpled up her empty bag from her belt loop and shoved it in her pocket, then turned away from the night market and set off in the direction of her street family.

Then, in spite of her hunger, in spite of the market smells that taunted her, for the first time in months, Kora looked down to search the sidewalk. The waning light revealed the dull black of a mussel shell, and she carefully picked it up to reveal its lavender-tinged, pearlescent inner coating. The edges had crumbled, but it was a small, fragile joy all the same. Kora pocketed it before walking home. When the constellations emerged in the darkening sky, the crushed shells on the ground glittered like diamonds.

SWEETHOPE FAIR

Die Booth

Every year, around midsummer, the music comes in loops and rags, flung by the wind from beyond the trees of Old Wen. Every year for as long as Len could remember, the fair had come to Sweethope. And every year Nana Enid would say, 'No, Len, you're not going.'

It wasn't that Enid was mean. She wasn't even strict, particularly. At any other time – unless he was meant to be in school – Len was left to roam the woods with more freedom than was usual even for a small village in the '70s. Their door was never locked: he came and went as he pleased, crafting empires in the undergrowth and back in time for tea. Yet, once a year, Enid would turn the key in the lock and pull a book from the high shelf, dropping it in a puff of dust in front of him at the kitchen table. 'Read.'

'I don't want to. It's for babies.'

'Read.' Enid said.

Len had liked the book more than he'd ever admit, but he didn't like it more than he'd like to be out there with the others, yelling blue murder on the rickety rides. Through the window, cracked open to let in the honeysuckle night, he could hear their screams, the voices mingling with the brash snatches of music, promising excitement so unknown that it was whetted to a glinting edge of fear. That's what the book made him feel. Fairy tales, bound in leather and with no author listed on the cover. Old. There were illustrations though. Pen and ink ones, conveying more menace than sketchy line drawings had any business doing. They'd fascinated him as deeply as any post-watershed film recorded from TV on grainy VHS, the ad breaks crammed with chat-lines, passed around the class at break times like contraband.

By the time Len reached his teens, the book no longer scared him and he was past being patient at missing out on Sweethope's annual social highlight.

'Read.'

'I've read it a million times.' Raising his voice at Nana still made him feel bad, but he was fast past caring. 'Don't talk to strangers. Don't tell them your name. Don't take anything from them, don't go with them – I get why you made me read this stuff when I was little, but I'm not a kid any more, Nan. Everyone from school is gonna be there. They all think I'm weird as it is!'

'Better they think you're weird than you turn up missing.' Enid pushed the book closer to him, with shaking hands.

Len closed his eyes, his knuckles digging into his forehead as he leaned on the table. 'Jenny Thorpe? That was one time, it was years ago.'

'And the time before that, and the time before that.' She leaned against the table, her head wagging. 'When's the next?'

'They weren't kidnapped, you know.' Len said. 'They ran away, and I don't blame them – anything's better than rotting in this bloody backwater.'

'Language, Leonard.' Enid's tone was more pitying than angry and somehow that made it worse. He banged his head against his clenched fists.

'It's not fair.'

'It's not *safe*.' She said it as if teenagers were going missing left, right and centre from every fair, and not one girl who ran away from her boring family ages ago. Maybe she thought there *were* more missing – she got confused about a lot of things these days. 'I tell you what. I'll give you a fiver to get the bus to Bettshill instead. You can go on Saturday. Go to the pictures or something. Get a hamburger.'

'It's not the same. I'll be on my own.'

'Take one of your friends.'

Len slammed the book shut with a heavy slap, dust glittering up from the cover in a shaft of sunlight. 'I don't *have* any friends, because you won't let me go to the fair.' He pushed back his chair and pushed away the book in one angry shove, standing. He was a head taller than Nana Enid now, and he was nearly sixteen. She couldn't stop him forever.

That was part of it, but not all. Len knew that he didn't have any friends because he was different, in ways too numerous to list. Too short, too quiet, too awkward, too serious. He could never tell when people were making fun of him or being friendly. The next year when the fair came, Nana Enid fell on the front path and he sat with her all night in A&E at Bettshill, before getting a taxi home alone. The year after that, she was living more in the past than the present, her eyes bright with memory, clouding over when they met his.

'You stay away from the fair, Lenny.'

'The fair's not until June, Nan.'

'You stay away!'

'I'm too old for the fair, now, Nan.'

Her expression softened, as if she was seeing him clearly for the first time in years. 'You should go out, with your friends.' She patted his hand with light fingers, then turned, looking for something. 'Where's my purse?'

'It's OK, Nan. You don't need your purse.'

'I'll give you a fiver, for the pictures.'

Len bit his lip. A familiar, stuffy feeling was building at the base of his throat. 'It's alright Nan. I'll go to the pictures another day.'

Enid looked at him hard. 'You're a good boy. You should meet a nice girl.'

'It's OK, Nan.' Len said, swallowing the feeling down. 'I don't want to meet a girl.'

When Nana Enid died, Len was twenty five. To go from looking after her to looking after the house just felt like the path of least resistance. He thought of selling up. Of moving on. He took a trip to Westonhough and visited a bar that had pictures of Marilyn and Liza and Bette on the walls. He sat alone with a pint until it was time to get the last train home. One year, a leaflet dropped through his letterbox printed in glossy rainbow colour, bundled up with the summer fair flyer. A parade in the city, on the same day as the Sweethope fair. He'd stared at it, for a long time, then crumpled them both into a ball and thrown them in the bin.

The years rolled into decades, turning faster than the cars of a Waltzer, until Len didn't notice any more. The village turned too – perhaps more slowly than the rest of the world, but still. They got broadband, and Len bought a laptop. He logged onto some special interest sites, the laptop screen a bright window in the curtained darkness of his bedroom, until he got too spooked by talk of data privacy and surveillance in the newspapers and went back to the confines of his own lonely imagination, homesick for a place he'd never been to.

It was on a website that he read the news.

'Sweethope teen missing from local funfair.' Scrolling down the busy page, Len clicked irritably away from pop-ups and adverts until he was faced with the smiling photograph of a boy. Michael Battersea, the story said, sixteen. He didn't recognise the kid from the village, but then he didn't get out quite as much as he used to. The boy's tousled dark hair and wry grin looked too happy to be missing. He wondered what his family were thinking. What they were going through. Whether every year they'd told Michael to stay away from the fair, just like Len had been told from the very first time he'd asked to go. He'd been thirteen when Jenny had disappeared. He remembered her still, with odd clarity for someone years older than him who he'd never really known, only seen around. Her blonde bob and keen green eyes were more defined in his memory now than Nana Enid's face. 1980, she'd gone. Then that other girl, Karen, in 1987 – he'd been twenty, then, and past the point of even really wanting to visit the fair, but Nana had gone on and on about that one: the Postman's daughter, only fifteen. Had there been others, like Nana had said? After she'd died, Len had stopped paying attention, but he thought he remembered village gossip and headlines in the free paper. A boy, maybe. Onscreen, Michael Battersea's placid smile mocked him, secretive and knowing. He opened a new window and typed into the browser: "Sweethope UK child disappearance".

He tried to forget. To dismiss it as so much fantasy, more like the tales still trapped like pressed flowers between the pages of the book left gathering dust on the top shelf in the kitchen. He'd not opened that book in thirty years, but those drawings still danced behind his eyes in dreams, taunting him with something just beyond his waking comprehension. But when seven years rolled around again, steady on their tracks as a Ghost Train, Len could not forget.

It felt stupid to call the police. He knew they'd laugh at him. What killer or kidnapper could operate for over a century? So, for the first time in his fifty-five years, Len Farley went to the Sweethope Fair.

Things travelled strangely when the fair was in town. Although he could hear the fairground tunes and even voices from the house, as soon as he set foot in Old Wen, the sounds just stopped. Emerging again from the wide belt of woodland that made up Old Wen, he found the bubble of light and noise uncanny after the silent embrace of the dark woods. What he was quite expecting, he wasn't sure, but it wasn't this. He'd thought it would be full of kids, but whilst there were plenty of young faces, he wasn't as out of place as he'd feared. He felt, strangely, unexpectedly, at home. It was both jarringly modern and eerily timeless. The thick stink of diesel and ten types of grease, hot engines chugging, fried food and a sizzling energy that made the hairs stand on Len's arms despite the warm night. But the music was the same music he'd listened to as a lonely teen – '70s and '80s pop hits, thudding so strongly from towers of speakers that he could feel every longing lyric like a slap to his chest. Even the gaudy décor looked thirty years out of date, the rides painted up in electric pink and blue and neon sunsets.

Suddenly, desperately, he needed a beer.

'Excuse me…' When the person he'd spoken to turned, for a moment Len's tongue failed him. He'd never been great with people, but he'd never been struck speechless by a woman's beauty before. She grinned at him like she knew, tilting her head as her round cheeks dimpled, grey hair fluffed up like a halo. 'Is there a…?' Concession stand? Pub? What were words? 'Beer tent, or something, do you know?'

'Over there, my lover.' He followed her pointing finger, and saw a stand, right there, serving drinks and snacks. How he'd missed it, he could not fathom.

'Thank–' She was gone. Len frowned. It was so warm out, he felt… unusual. Just the heat, and nerves, certainly: a drink would help. He joined the queue to the stand, gazing around at life finally happening.

The fair folk were *all* beautiful. He didn't know how that was possible, when there was such a wide range of looks between them, as if the carnival had travelled the world ten times over and picked up stowaways from every place and walk of life. Even the men who looked like him – ageing, balding, their waistlines spreading – held a radiance that made him wonder if what he saw in the mirror was really so terrible, or if that was just another lie he'd been taught by the outside world to swallow whole. It was clear as starlight to him now, why so many youngsters had stayed with the fair when it moved on: just being here made him feel lighter. So carefree that he could save any mourning for his lost visits until he was back in a home that now felt like it had never been real in the first place.

'Take your order, mate?' Len turned back. The man behind the counter had a shaved head, flawless dark brown skin and a smile even more dazzling than the woman who'd directed him there. 'What do you need?'

'Oh. Sorry.' Len tripped over his words, realised he'd been staring. 'Miles away.' The vendor was still smiling, warm and sincere and not an ounce mocking. 'A beer, please.' There wasn't much selection, nothing he recognised from any shop, the bottles labelled like home-brew: *cider, beer, mead, wine,* described in looping ink handwriting. Perhaps that was normal, for fairs. Perhaps now, he was the type of man who went to them. The thought caught inside him, swelling warm with the noise and the night air, the reek of hot sugar and cigarette smoke. 'And some candy floss.' He nodded at the back shelf, feeling reckless, and the man handed him a plastic bag full of pink stuff. 'Thank you.'

'You are so welcome.' He took Len's coins with a wide smile and it was all Len could do to tear himself away.

The beer was fine. Weak, but it had been cheap, so he wasn't about to complain. Len floated on the tide of the crowd, the world rocking like a ship, the wind waves. Expanding inside, his heart and lungs were bubbles, rising. He wanted to laugh, for nothing more than the sheer joy of freedom, as the saturated lights beat bright around him. He'd never eaten candy floss before, and he wasn't too sure of it. It was cloying, tacking his fingers together in a familiar way he couldn't quite place, yet tasted of nothing but sweetness, melting away but lingering. Sucking his fingers, Len looked around, dazed into the night. Heat thick as incense, like being submerged in blood. The air was waiting. A held breath before a scream. And there, he caught someone else's eye.

'You.' The same grin. 'I know you.' In the photograph his hair had looked dark, but in the revolving lights of the Carousel it was ginger. The boy smiled. Not a day older than sixteen. Len had to be wrong: the beer was stronger than he'd thought, from how his head was spinning, and kids all look the same these days. From the crowd, a girl danced, and took the boy by the hand. Sweetness sealed Len's lips, choking him. Blonde hair and green eyes. Blue mascara and the same ABBA t-shirt that had been stitched into Len's memory for four decades. 'Jenny?' His voice croaked out even stranger to him than these ghosts. Her smile was pure mischief as she gave him a little wave, and he felt his legs buckle.

'You're alright, mate.'

'I think I've had too much to drink.' Len said, as he was led away, a strong hand at his elbow barely holding him up.

'Of that stuff? I doubt it.' An arm snaked around his waist and Len clung to his beer bottle like a lifebuoy. The voice close to his ear was low and rolling as the tide of breeze in the trees. Its owner chuckled, and goosebumps stuttered up Len's nape, like iron filings in the pull of a magnet, as he leaned heavily into the warm presence at his side.

Midges danced in the lowering light like sparks. Leaves backlit all the colours of the rainbow, more vibrant than the fairground lights they were leaving behind. Len looked around, faltering. 'Where are we going?'

'Out of the noise for a bit. You alright?'

He still couldn't get a proper look at the man at his side, but quiet sounded good. Len nodded. 'Yeah. Thanks. Who are you?' It felt like an odd question to ask, as if he wasn't a grown adult in full control of his life.

Somehow, he felt the man smile. 'Jack. Green. And you are?'

'Len.'

'I'm glad to meet you, Len.'

The shiver was back, trickling across Len's scalp in a surge of sensation. Ivy-twined trees steepled above towering spears of foxglove that throbbed neon. The air smelled fermented, like ale or mead. The scent of wild garlic. Honeysuckle. Nettles. A wet slap of perfume overwhelming his senses in dizzy pulses. By the time they stopped, leaning against the wide trunk of a massive oak, Len realised that he could no longer see the lights or hear the noise of the fair. That he had no idea how far they had walked. That he had no idea who Jack was.

'I feel–' The words failed, unsaid, as he turned to look at his rescuer and found he couldn't. Jack stood right there before him, but Len's gaze refused to fully settle on him, as if his eyes didn't quite know what to see and glanced off whenever he tried to focus. The shape of a man. The suggestion of a face, kaleidoscoping in feature and shape, a swirling darkness at its core, indistinct and unknowable.

Don't look them in the eye.

Don't thank them, or you'll owe them.

Don't eat or drink anything they give you.

He should have been afraid. Years spent trapped in safety, yet that's what felt like danger to him then, like death. 'What have you given me?' He looked wildly at his beer, the foreign taste thick in his throat. The bottle fell from his fingers, hitting the mossy ground with a quiet thump.

Jack said, 'The truth.' He tilted his head, the flicker of features slowing to a handsome face with a deeply etched smile. His hair receded back from a high forehead and hung around his shoulders in ashy drifts. His beard was long and grey, a lighter flash striping down the centre of his chin. From beneath heavy dark brows he watched keenly with eyes of molten glass, black and liquid and holding all the heat of the dying sun.

Beneath Len's palms the bark of the tree writhed, and scintillated with colour like an opal. The threat, all this time, had been freedom. 'You're not really a man, are you?'

'No?' Jack's smile tilted, so sweet and amused that Len couldn't find it in himself to care anymore. How was this truth any less true than the bland years alone? 'Am I not?' Taking Len's hand, he guided it, gently enough that Len knew he could pull away at any point. Thought about pulling away. Didn't. His senses spun, reeling, a different kind of light-headed to the candy floss high. A blood-rush swoop, thudding in his pulse points like an answering howl, not learned but known, the dull yearning of decades sharpening fit to split his soul in two.

'Alright. You're a man.'

'So what are you gonna do about it?'

I don't know. The words balanced on the brink of voicing. But they were lies. He *did* know. He'd known for years. Leaning in, they met, his lips parting to let Jack lick the lost time from

31

his tongue like liquid sugar. Kissing him breathless, Len chased his lips, sleepy-eyed and panting. It was almost too good: he could handle it only in small sips, like that crafty fairground beer, intoxicating and lifesaving. When they parted, he could only stare. The sweet relief of an empty head, the heady rush of surrender. Jack asked, 'Are you scared?'

'Not anymore.' Len said, and it was true. He let himself be led, down into the sweet grass patched to pale gold and drowsing with flies. Gazed enchanted as Jack butterflied a kiss to the hot flutter of his pulse at his throat, at his temples, at each wrist.

'You'll stay.' This arcane creature, holding his desires to ransom.

Don't go to the fair. You'll be taken by a fairy.

And Len *wants*. Something to fill up the longing hollow echo of decades with light and noise and devastating touch. To quench the need to be taken. To be *taken care of.*

Even when you have no choice, are you truly a prisoner, if you're willing? If, given that choice, you'd stay anyway? He met Jack's mirror gaze and the world outside Old Wen dispersed to a whisper.

Sunset dipped the woods in gold, solitary trees lit up like a theatre set, a backdrop to their play. Time slumbered, and the quiet sky turned to mother-of-pearl. Where it once was *him*, now it was *them*, for as long as they might last. Maybe forever. Who back in the ordinary world could offer that? An eternity dreaming, learning one another line by line until they could write their own poetry on the close, breathless pages of the night.

SHROPS LIVE – 2ND AUGUST 2022

UPDATED 17 HOURS AGO

by Colin Thorpe

Police are appealing for the public's help to find a missing man from Sweethope.

Leonard Farley, 55, was last seen at around 9am on Saturday, June 25th at the village corner shop, wearing dark trousers, a light-coloured short-sleeved shirt and black baseball cap.

Mr Farley lives alone and is known to frequent the areas around Sweethope and Bettshill.

Inspector Craig Hollis said: 'We are very concerned for Leonard's welfare and are appealing for the help of the public in finding him.

'I would urge anyone who may have seen Leonard or anyone with any information about his whereabouts to please get in touch by calling Bettshill Police on 999 or via our website, quoting incident number 4658342.'

AMERICAN SHORT FICTION, 1800-1999

Aran Kelly

In the library we were talking about those old American names. 'Jebediah,' she said. 'You don't hear that any more. Imagine looking at a baby and thinking, "Ah, Jebediah."'

By "any more" she meant in the period of fiction we were currently examining, the early twentieth century short story writers: Hemingway, Fitzgerald, Langston Hughes. Every name that appeared in the text, we wrote down. Between us and the rest of the people assigned to this project we were going through almost every book in the library, which was essentially every book in existence. So, we were reasonably sure that we had covered every name – first names only, of course.

I didn't want the project to end. I had become accustomed to entering the library in the mornings, marking the heavy leather-bound register, and walking through the long desks that lined the room like pews to my seat across from her. The desks were constructed of an old grainy wood that was very satisfying to run my fingers across. There was a musty smell of old books to the library that was unlike anywhere else in the city. We would take the day's books from the pile beside the desk and begin. A shaft of sunlight from a window high in the reading balcony above us slowly travelled from one side of the library to the other, and we knew it was time to go home when it came to land on our desk.

We worked in unison when we started to tire. One of us read the names out loud as we found them and the other would write them on the list. I liked it when she was reading most of all. I liked listening to her voice echo tentatively in the wide-open library. I liked it when she decided to digress for a moment from simply reading names, and would read out a sentence or two of prose that she found particularly beautiful. We were good partners.

We could talk to each other a little without fear of disturbing anyone else, since the only other one in the room with us was the American. He was a tall, heavyset, red-faced man, who wore the same dusty blazer every single day. Every morning he would stalk around the entire room three times, then set himself down at a desk, a different one every day, and take out all his papers and spread them over the desk assertively. He would always position himself facing the door so he could glare at whoever came in – usually me, since I arrived after him, and I took this as a personal affront until I realised he would also glare at the representative of the Bureau every time they arrived.

He would mutter to himself as he bent over his texts and jabbed names into his sheets. The American's remit was US non-fiction. They had given it to him to work on alone, which seemed to me like an excessively large project for one person.

Any time we offered help he rebuffed us, so eventually we stopped asking.

We got along relatively well, the three of us, but she and I made sure not to say anything too critical about America in his presence. Not because we'd offended him before, but because of the way he spoke about his home. I could never pin down exactly what state he came from – and I suppose it didn't matter – but it was somewhere with tall purple mountain ranges, wide open blue skies, and a forest path that led out to a lake that glimmered in the morning sun. He seemed to depart from us entirely when he was talking about this place, staring into the distance at something a million miles away. He seemed to think he would be able to return there someday.

We were not to make contact with the people in the other rooms – our work was supposed to remain separate, to not overlap in any manner. The only other person we ever saw was the representative of the Bureau, someone different every week. All the representatives wore the same jet-black blazer and immaculately clean dress shoes, and they would wrinkle their nose as they ran a fingertip across the dust on the doorframe, as though they expected us to keep the place in good order. They handed out our assignments, helped us find the requisite literature for the next week, and collected any completed sheets. By the end of autumn, they were warning us on each visit to conserve our ink and paper, unnecessarily – we were aware that those were non-renewable resources.

What we were getting out of the arrangement was food, fresh clothing, things like that. Necessities. They also promised us money, whenever money became important again, but privately

I did not believe that day would ever come. For me, at least, it was fine to simply have something to do. She had some other non-material goal, though we never discussed such things.

If I had to give her a title, like the American's, I suppose she would just have been the partner. Or my partner. Because we were partners – first as colleagues, sifting through words together, then as friends. Later I wondered if this was why the Bureau took her away, when she disappeared.

The best time was the winter, when we had no choice but to stay in the library. It would have been too harsh, the weather, for us to journey from our homes in the morning and back at night. I didn't miss my home, with the smell of damp, the rats in the basement, and the biting cold that cut through the walls of my bedroom. The heating in the library didn't work, but it was still well-insulated and had avoided most of the bombing. By night we would climb to the windows in the attic and watch the snow falling in the moonlight to land like a heavy blanket of ash on the burnt-out buildings. Even the American settled a little in the winter and would eat with us in the mornings. I didn't know where he lived for the rest of the year.

One winter night she and I were lying in our sleeping bags on the floor beside our desk and quietly talking about what names we'd like if we ever got to pick our own. 'Henry,' I said. 'Good and sturdy. It seems like a Henry always knew where he stood.'

She thought for a bit and said, 'To me, Sarah has a weightless quality to it. Like it could take flight at any moment and go wherever it wished. Try it, sound it out. Do you see what I mean?' She was right; the sound of it seemed to soar up towards the rafters, to the moonlit window and out beyond sight.

I envied her ability to hold on to her sense of herself. I wondered how she would fare when the rebuilding was complete. In the final days I regretted not saying any of this to her, but I was not capable then.

Winter took us past the mid-twentieth century in our short fiction and into the post-war era. This wasn't my favourite period; I was still stuck on the 1920s. Look at this list of names from a Fitzgerald story: Charlie, George, Paul, Alix, Claude. It went on like that. Very international. A big step up from the earlier works, the Nathaniel Hawthornes and such, which I was dreading going back to, to Hawthorne's novels, when we would finish with short stories and change over to novels, because then who knew around what corner you might find a Jebediah.

Around this time, I discovered that the American was hiding things in the library. Small things: pieces of string, a flashlight, a pocketknife. He hid them on bookshelves, under desks, in far corners of the upper balcony. Once, I noticed a disturbed floorboard and carefully pried it up; underneath was an almost complete box of DIY tools. I did not know what he intended to achieve through this hoarding. Was it to establish control? The library was not a place where such things applied.

She and I spoke of the places we were reading about that we would like to visit, if we were able. She said one day she would visit these places. Hawthorne's New England. Capote's New York. Hemingway's Spain. 'The Snows of Kilimanjaro'. All the rest. It was wishful thinking. She wasn't the same as the American; she didn't really think she could go anywhere else but here. At least, anywhere very far away from here. We were, in truth, going to be stuck here for a long time. We were not even supposed to be reading the stories very closely. It was names only that the Bureau wanted.

The spring was bad for the American. It wasn't good for any of us – anyone could see we were running out of pens, that the ink pots were running low, that the project was at risk. But it hit him worst of all. He muttered to himself more and more and knocked out staccato rhythms on his desk with empty biro pens. He started dragging his desk around the floor to follow the shaft of sunlight as it progressed through the day.

Once he came up to us, to our desk, and threatened us with his pocketknife. 'I know what you say about my nation,' he hissed. 'I know you're stealing paper. Is this the kind of fool you take me for?' Neither of us responded or looked up; we knew his threats of violence were empty. He was harmless. He was deluded. He thought he could go home.

Early in the spring she disappeared. One day she was there and the next she wasn't. I arrived in the morning to the American's glare, but no sight of my partner. The American said she hadn't been there when he came in. I asked the representative of the Bureau the next time they appeared, but they simply said it was above their station. For a time I was upset, I will admit. It was difficult to focus on my books, and I would constantly look to the door, expecting her to walk in at any moment. Eventually, I got back on track. As the days went on and she did not return, it became clear that there wasn't anything I could do about it. I had to leave it to the Bureau and get on with the work.

Around this time, the Bureau left us. The visits stopped being weekly, became monthly, and then we just didn't see anyone again. Perhaps they ran out of resources, or everyone had just died. Either was equally possible. Without anyone to take them away, the lists began to pile up. Stacks of paper climbed the walls to the ceiling, to the point that when a list was finished, one had to climb the stairs to the upper balcony and carefully place the sheet atop the pile. The American and I were very careful not to knock them over. It became very important for us to build them as high as possible. It gave us something to focus on.

We were not being paid anymore, and we had to scavenge our own food from the nearby shops. Not me; I didn't leave the library any more. It was home now, and I did not see how going out into the open could be safe for me. We still had no contact with the other people in the library, and part of me feared what would happen if they ever came into our room. I relied on the American, who would go out and come back with any canned goods he could find, or anything else we deemed safe to eat. He was happy to do it; this type of work suited him far better. Once the shops ran dry, he began breaking into the abandoned houses around the city centre. One day he came back with a bundle of papers and placed them on the desk before me.

'Did you know she lived nearby?' From his blazer he produced a framed photograph of a woman standing with her arm around a man I did not know. The woman was my partner – much younger, her clothes in better condition, her face less tight and worn. 'And all these papers were at the back of a cabinet in the kitchen. Recent.'

The papers bore the letterhead of the library and were written on front and back. They were indeed dated recently. As I

41

shifted through them it became clear that they were a series of unsent love letters written in beautiful flowing language, describing a great love, a deep love, a love that persisted through disaster and ruin. In fact, they read like some of the stories we were reading, the particularly lovely ones, the ones that had a particular grasp of language that reached for something greater.

I asked the American to take the papers away – to either throw them out or to see at least if he could use them to write some of his names on. We were running out of paper, you see, and now it was clear why; she had taken so much for her own use. I kept the photograph on my desk as my work moved into the 1990s. In moments of distraction I would look at it and wonder about the people in it. Where they were now. Where she was now.

The American was also upset by the letters, that paper had been taken from the project, but the project meant something different to him than it did to me. He took the disappearance of the Bureau much harder than I did. To me it was not a disaster, but the Bureau to him meant the promise of a thing he had once and had lost, life in the imperial core, and he yearned for it to come back, yet I, I didn't have any of it, he was fifty-five years old and memory for him was a dangerous trap to fall into.

The American had to be stopped when he came in with matches and gasoline to burn the place down. Well, I don't know whether he wanted to burn the entire building or simply the lists. In either case it would have been unacceptable, so I stopped him. I don't want to talk about how.

After that it was only me. I still did not see anyone else in the entire building. I went to search for them and found myself walking through large empty echoing rooms, with bare bookcases and feral cats nesting under the desks. Maybe there were still people elsewhere; they may have been in another room. It was a large library. I could not have been the only person still dedicated to the project.

Not long after the American was disposed of I ran out of paper completely, but the work had to continue. It was beyond matters of payment or survival or rebuilding now. However, I could not bring myself to write on the surface of the library. It was more than a place of work; it was a sacred space. The bookcases were icons of my faith, the desks my altars, the books themselves the source of the names – I could not defile them with my work. I began to write the names on my body. I had to press down very hard on my skin to make sure that the ink would stay in place. I stopped washing, stopped wearing clothes that would rub off the ink and sat there naked amongst the towering stacks of paper. Eventually, the ink ran out too. I took a quill, sharpened it and then dug into my skin, carving bloody letters, dragging the point carefully in tiny letters across my canvas. The cuts quickly scarred, making me a living archive, a flesh tome.

I went searching for food, to see if the American had hidden any secret stockpiles from me, and instead found where he'd left the letters. They were on a bookshelf, tucked between the covers of the collected works of Edgar Allen Poe. To my surprise, he had not written on them. His lack of dedication to the project, I thought. Then I sat down and spread them over the dark wooden floor, and bent over them. A cut on my forehead reopened and blood slowly dripped on her words, but still I was able to read. This time I spent a very long time with the letters. I sat with her prose until I could see the truth of it. I had been too dismissive previously. I still did not know who these letters were intended for, but it would be a crime to let them go unanswered.

For the first time in months, I went outside. I climbed up to the roof where the midday sun was blazing and as I dragged my slashed soles along the bare broiling concrete the bloody streaks congealed immediately, heavy tracks of deep crimson trailing me to the edge of the building. I looked towards the white ball in the clear blue sky, and in the sheer glare for a moment some figure flashed in my vision, a remnant of memory, an echo of a dark morning sitting at the desk across from her, a face I had not forgotten. I had to reciprocate the letters and so I took a sharp stone from the gravel to make sure that the last name I wrote would be hers.

AS LIGHT, UNRAVELING

Brianna Cunliffe

There is a jar by the river. In the jar is a small brown note-book and a ballpoint pen. In the jar is a question, and answers, tangling, festering, growing.

I find it on a Thursday, staggering to a rest on a long run, sneakers spattered with mud. The freak March sunshine has barely cleared the trail of snow, leaving it a minefield of sucking goop and stubborn ice patches, freeing the pond to roar more wildly to its headwaters, passing under the creaking bridge.

The signs declare the town commons a Drug-Free Zone. Threats of extra penalties are routinely ignored by students lighting up along the slowly unfreezing reservoir. The crooked footbridge and the path through the pine-needles approximate wilderness, though the roofs of houses are just visible through the treetops and puttering engines occasionally break through the forest quiet and the sound of rushing water.

I clamber down to the riverbed, grit my teeth against the cold water to wipe the mud from my palms, and an unnatural glint catches my eye. There, tucked against the post of the bridge, sits a small glass jar, with a small brown notebook and a ballpoint pen.

Drying my hands on my pant leg, I reach for it, trying to discern its purpose – if it's some sort of experiment, something I should leave undisturbed, but the lid unlatches easily, and on the front of the notebook, there is a request, written in large, messy letters, vaguely child-like.

TELL ME A STORY.

I flip open the lid, a smile brushing my lips despite myself. People have. There are dozens of entries all scrawled in the broad fluidity of the same pen. *Once upon a time. Once upon a time. It was a dark and stormy night. In the beginning, there was darkness. For God so loved the world–*

Entries fly past my eyes, retellings from the clumsy to the heartfelt. Old wives' tales, Disney movies. Things that go bump in the night. A different alphabet jolts me out of an easy reading trance, and I struggle to identify it. Hindi, maybe. There are others that I'm more sure of. Russian. Chinese. Arabic. More languages than you'd expect in a small Maine town. The international students at the college, maybe.

But I would bet good money that translated, these stories in their varied tongues would begin like any of the others. *Once upon a time.*

The next page is blank: it's my turn. The chattering woodpeckers feel like an audience, like I'm a child onstage inhaling before her one line of song in some play. I'm writing before I've even consciously chosen the story:

There once was a woman who dwelled in the sea, until her skin was stolen from her, and she was confined to the land by the one that claimed to love her.

The selkie story. My mother's favourite. The grown-up's fantasy of the changeling, a beautiful way to excuse away this unbelonging that cut like a dull knife. We are not of this place, not really, and so this unhappiness is only natural. It would vanish, if only we could find that skin, break the love that bound and slip, soundless, back, beneath the waves.

I choose the ending she always chooses. The one that's closest to happy. The one that ends with the selkie-wife finding her skin while her husband is away and getting free. *She embraces the sea like a lover,* I write, *and goes, at last back home.*

The literary flourish makes me blush, embarrassed though I am alone. I close the notebook quickly, like some bully might read over my shoulder and taunt me for my airs. *Like a lover, indeed,* I taunt myself. *Someone needs to break a dry spell.*

Ridiculous or not, the words are on the page. With a little sense of loss, I replace the notebook in the jar, and – my hand hesitates. A contented hum seems to exhale from the page, a sound like a faint bell, lingering a bit longer than it should when the pen clicks back in the jar.

But I'm imagining things. It wouldn't be the first time.

Phantom deer, barking dogs, roots rising up to trick me. The mind looks for excuses for the scraped and battered knees, the constant heartbeat of anxious fear. That's what my father always told me, told us both, my mother and I, in that tone he always thought was comforting and that just made me want to drive a pike through my own hand, ask if that was the sort of excuse he meant.

I dust the dirt from my knees, leave the jar where I found it, unsteady, swept in the sound of the river flowing. Women stolen from the sea and their vengeful rattling of the trunk drift in my head as my feet pound the pavement all the way home.

Fickle spring has vanished when I come to the river again, breath fogging in clouds over the frozen mud, but the jar remains. The notebook, though, has changed: a new question scrawled across its cover.

WHAT'S A LITTLE THING THAT BROKE YOUR HEART?

I page through, surprised at the abundance of entries. It's only been a few days, and the pages are almost full, like passerby couldn't wait to get it off their chests. *Changing his name in my phone,* someone had written, a frowny face adorning the entry. A different writer: *When she wouldn't hold my hand in public.* They kept coming.

When my son stopped letting me tie his shoes for him.

They took down the tree I prayed beneath to build another ugly house.

My grandmother called me by her sister's name, near the end, asking me why I'd left her alone.

Little things. There are a thousand I could choose. But something about the weight of the little book in my hand, stuffed to its brim with scrawled anecdotes, confessions, tirades, goodbyes – something about it moves me, tripping a vague memory somewhere behind the curtain of my conscious mind.

Reading the sorrows here in these pages, I write. *Leaving them with you.*

You? My hand hesitates above the word, and I move to scratch it out, then justify. *You,* the reader of the notebook. *You,* the person who left the jar. The writer of the questions. That's what I mean. Of course. What else?

But the paper seems to lift a bit, around the word, to warm against my skin. The empty jar glinting in the cold white winter light, a strange resonance pouring from the mouth, like a space ripe for an echo, the wet rim of a crystal glass, waiting to sing.

Leaving them with you. It no longer feels like a sentiment. It feels, as I replace the notebook in the jar, like an apology. Like a promise.

My steps start to drag me to the foot of the bridge like clockwork every day.

WHAT'S THE FARTHEST YOU'VE EVER FELT FROM HOME?

I answer on a Tuesday, wondering if it knows I've been feeling lonely. To this notebook and this notebook only, I admit unhappiness with this independence that was once my dream. It feels like I've thrown a fistful of sun into some festering corner, unclogged some drain deep within me, making way for– I don't know. For something. Something new. A different kind of story.

Wednesday.

WHEN DID YOU REALISE YOUR PARENTS WEREN'T INVINCIBLE?

Way too early, I write, and a half-guilty laugh rolls through me. *When I made my own peanut butter sandwiches from age five on. Killing spiders because Mom was always too petrified.*

Thursday. I find myself anticipating it, wondering what the question will be today, composing my hypothetical answers.

49

It's not that strange, I tell myself. I'd be coming here anyway, for my run. I just think it's interesting, whatever public art project or collective history or social experiment this is. I write to provide data.

WHAT LESSON DID YOU
HAVE TO UNLEARN?

As if I had wisdom to give. As if someone really wanted to know.

My pen eats away one page, then another, then another. I write things I've never told anyone, things I've never even admitted to myself. Leaving, I am lighter, each time I replace the lid on that strange little jar, knowing it will be here, new again, tomorrow, patient, consistent, really, truly listening.

Maybe I just like having someone to talk to. And what's wrong with that?

Friday it pours, the kind of cold, miserable rain no one in their right mind would be out in unless they have to.

I go anyway.

I pull my arms from my raincoat, drape it over my body and the jar like some strange tent, peer at the notebook in the half-dark I've created to protect it from the steady rain.

TELL ME ABOUT YOUR BEST BIRTHDAY.

Me? The pronoun registers, vaguely unsettling, as if the notebook has delusions of grandeur about sentience, or that its planter was whispering somewhere from behind the trees. Me. I'd called it you. But before it could give me pause, I am putting the pen to paper.

I write about the time I turned ten at the roller rink, when I told everyone to bring cans for the food drive and they brought me presents anyway. Or maybe I write about my fifteenth, jumping in the creek with Lila and Bea and getting chased off by the neighbours. I couldn't quite remember, later that night, as I turned my key in the door, and the fact that I couldn't remember didn't bother me quite as much as it should have.

Saturday. The river glitters, high with yesterday's rains, and people crowd the trailhead, braving the muck for the rarity of the warm sun. Still, I find seclusion, resting my back against the bridge's trestle and waiting until the last of the voices fade before popping the lid of the jar.

WHO IS YOUR HERO? DO YOU HAVE ONE?

I struggle for a moment to make sense of what I see. The letter "h" in hero is just ever so vaguely wrong, a little too jagged, like it's gotten stuck in a funhouse mirror. It looks like a child's handwriting.

The other questions fail to visualise, as I struggle to remember if the script had been the same each time. Maybe. Maybe not. But it certainly hadn't been this halting scrawl.

A memory flits across my vision, wavery and uncertain, of being charmed by an entry yesterday, or the day before. A brief, sincere entry in the weird, wiry writing of a child still trying to master the shapes. Writing that looked a lot like the one now on the front of the notebook. The writing of–

The uneasy question rises up in my mind, unnerving because I'd never thought to ask it: who was the owner of the jar, the asker of questions, the reader of stories? I'd just accepted its reality, this small, simple instrument in this inconspicuous spot on this poorly-travelled path, never bothering to interrogate intent. The threads fail to come together, under close inspection. Why here, why this? Who? There is a child involved, clearly, sometimes participant, sometimes leader. Some sort of supervised art project, a collaborative endeavour, maybe a homeschool's outreach?

I shake it off. Maybe there are cameras, somewhere in the brush, and I'll be on *Good Morning America*, talking about what a wonderful way it is to bring people together.

I cannot think of any heroes. Not a single one. I wish I could apologise, to the child, for my shortcoming. But I can only put pen to paper. Again and again, day after day.

I begin to forget what I have written as soon as I write it. It slides out of my mind as I close the lid of the jar. I try to recall what the question even was, behind the wheel of my car returning through the Maine coastline mist, and nearly veer off the road when I cannot.

The recollection like a black hole, a purposefully blurred photograph, unnerves me. I keep seeing the child's writing, hearing it, like a voice, strange and echoing in the glass confines, beside the rushing river. *Tell me a story. Tell me a story.*

I stay away, for a while. I take some overtime at work, drink warm, flat beer in some dive bar with my incorrigibly friendly coworker, knowing he wants to take me home, knowing I will smile politely and say I have an early morning and must be going now. I clean out my closets, my drawers, scrub at the baseboards, the stubborn stains of the shower tile grout. I tell myself I am diverted, productive, unperturbed.

But I feel a little bit like the selkie wife, pawing through the house while her husband is away, looking for her skin.

So I go back, and there it is: the glint of the jar and the heady rush it summons, Pavlovian, salivating at the expected release of – what? General emotion, bottled trauma, petty resentment, the introvert's secret need to be listened to, the ego craving the stroke of attention? Whatever it is, I am hungry for more. The jar seems to hum as I pop the lid, and the thought skitters through my mind like a half-seen infestation. It is hungry for me, too.

I hold back from looking at the question, stretching out the anticipation, its pleasure, for one more second. In this potential space, anything could be asked of me. Each of the thousand stories trembling to get out of my throat could be set free.

Exhaling, I look down.

HAVE YOU BROKEN A PROMISE LATELY?

The question is scrawled across the entire face of the notebook, in massive, frantic letters. And this time I can't explain it away, can't claim it's just a parent and their kid or an art class at one of the high schools. Because this time, it's my handwriting.

HAVE YOU BROKEN A PROMISE LATELY?

I throw the pen into the river, resist the urge to heave my stomach's contents over the railing after it, as the open mouth of the jar gapes at me. HAVE YOU HAVE YOU HAVE YOU–

My penmanship. Messy, looping, unmistakable. The bane of teachers' existence. My hand. My voice, in some strange static way, echoing out of this strange mirror, sitting

53

there, waiting for me. HAVE YOU BROKEN HAVE YOU BROKEN BROKEN–

I have to know. I have to know what it is. What it wants. What it wants with me.

I miss one shift at work. Another. The days slide past, pooling into sameness, clouds clustering and breaking overhead like a time lapse. Passerby shuffle quickly past me, as if I'm the dangerous one, the strange one. And maybe I am, huddled in my dark jacket crouched on the banks of the river, staring at a jar, daring it to move. I haven't opened it, not since, so in my mind, it's still those same words, blaring out a kind of accusation in my own script:

HAVE YOU BROKEN A PROMISE LATELY?

The pen is back. I have a sneaking suspicion that I could burn the notebook to cinders, shatter the jar to dust, and the next day it would still be there, glinting, glinting. But I have been here watching, for…

Not a single soul has approached it. No casual writers happening on it by chance, no tenders, no one there to swap out covers or collect the writings. Maybe there never was. There is only the jar, glinting, winking at me. A PROMISE. A PROMISE.

Like some sort of clandestine biologist of the not-quite living, hoping if I linger long enough it will reveal its true nature. It does not move, but my thoughts do, churning over all the stories I'd told it, this it, whatever it is, trying to find some common thread, some purpose to it, but I keep running up against the absurd tenderness of the questions, like the lover you'd always dreamed of, wanting to know you down to the very core. But not *you*, not *you* only. Us. All of us.

It is learning me. Learning us. We are feeding it. Gathering these scraps of lives – and for what? Senseless anecdotes, impotent, disregarded even by ourselves.

I'd written about my birthday, for crying out loud. The one where– the one where–

I can't remember.

My heart tumbled like a stone down a canyon. Which birthday had it been? No matter. What else? I'd written about my mother's favourite story. The woman who– something about the sea. The woman–

I can't remember.

I can't remember any of it.

Horror snags like a fishhook in my gut, and rips me, jagged, open. It is feeding *on me.* Where else would the memory go? Eaten. Eaten, by whatever this thing was, trapped in its jar, reaching its tendrils out to anyone willing to pour their heart out over pen and paper. All it took was a question and a glint of glass in the sun. A charming idiosyncrasy. An irredeemable theft.

Perhaps there are dozens of jars by rivers. Dozens of hapless, lonely people, feeding this thing their stories, afternoon after afternoon.

As if it senses my condemnation, my resolve, the jar hums, and maybe I have learned it, as it has learned me, for I hear it like a word. A word that tells me something is coming.

Dusk falls, banishing the pleasure-seekers and wholesome old couples with dogs with its chill. River rushes, emboldened by the last of the snowmelt. We are alone.

The jar begins to ring. Not like before, faint and effervescent. A deep, resonant toll, like those from steeples for a funeral, for a birth, for a coronation. Insistent sound that demands

55

witness. So I sit, my eyes wild and feral things as the jar at last cracks open and a web of light spills out.

It crawls like a living thing, draping itself over the empty air, undulating into a shape – like a child curled into the fetal position, plaintive whispers blinking out from the blue nodes of light and their flickering bridges between, some pinprick small and some swollen and bulbous as if they might burst. The figure rocks, back and forth, back and forth. I can see the whitecaps of the river through the vibrating, fragile constellation of its form. I can hear it keening, like a lost animal, like a frightened child, tremors of energy ricocheting from node to node, a constant hum rising and falling in pitch.

I reach out a single trembling finger, unable to stop myself, and touch the trembling sphere on the shoulder, the one that looks like a raindrop on the verge of rolling down a windowpane. It meets my skin, warm as any breathing creature, and the voice whispers into my ear, *He would break the apples apart with his bare hands, and we would eat even the seeds.*

I stumbled back, as the voice went on, and then, shaking, reached for another. *Mama told me no Prince Charming worth his salt would ever drive a pickup truck. Guess she was right.*

I turned sixteen during a thunderstorm and we ran barefoot to set off fireworks, trying to beat the lightning at its own game. A miracle we didn't get struck dead.

The stories. The stories. They're all here, all of these, hundreds, wrapped in this vague approximation of a body, this trembling imitation, play-acting at humanity.

Mine. The thought cuts through the wonder, the attempt to make out the words, the visions of the absent speakers. Mine Where are mine?

Can I take them back?

I reach and reach and reach, tripping the spheres like strings of a heart. But one doesn't stop when another begins; they play on and on, in infinite loops, the overlap growing. In the span of a dozen the sound becomes unintelligible, unbearable, but still, I cannot stop myself, and so my hands tear at the web of light, grasping, grasping at these varied flares, again and again, until the cacophony of voices radiating from disparate points, building and mounting and the mounting threatens to blot out reality, all the words running together, all the sense vanished, only a desperate insistence to be heard.

'Stop,' I say, senseless, unable even to hear it, to feel it leave my throat, so great the din, but I cannot unring the bell, cannot raise the dam again, can only plead, can only–

STOP, I scrawl in the notebook. STOP. STOP. STOP. Again, and again, until the pages tear, and it turns its almost head towards me, empty spaces devoid of light where the eyes ought to be. An unfinished, hungry, constellation.

The voices slough away into an unnatural silence that I feel in the hollows of my teeth.

The web of light hisses back into the mouth of the jar, and inside it, the ink begins to run from its sides, seeming to pour, to pour from thin air, a collection of syllables hissing like steam from a vent, bubbling, coalescing into–

My breath rasps in my hoarse throat. The tiny form of a fetus, almost translucent, an embryo bathed in that undulating sea of light and trapped sound and story.

The not-yet-born being turns its head and looks at me through the cracked jar.

I take the stories I have left and run.

I go home to my parents, abandoning the adult job I'd never liked that much and the apartment where the faucet had always leaked, locking the door and just driving, driving, driving far from the river and the jar and everything I have seen, and I try to forget.

At home I sleep for days and days, and then I walk alone for a long time, by the coastline, so empty in the late autumn chill, until the silhouette arrests me where I stand. It had been such a long time. I had forgotten.

There is a mailbox by the sea.

It has been there ever since I was a child. I had written in it, even then, my parents, by my side, occasionally scrawling their own brief notes. Closing the box, raising the flag, as if some pelagic postman had to be notified to come pick it up. There were notebooks piled on notebooks, dating back decades, pages filled to the brim. The mailbox was stuffed with stories.

And it pulls at me, stronger than the jar's vague magnet ever had, stronger than I knew how to withstand, until I kneel in the sand, my forehead pressed to the creaking box, and I file back through the salt-crusted, mildewing pages of the oldest journals, flicking through the senseless notes until I find it:

My own writing, a cautious child, fifteen years ago.

DO YOU EVER GET LONELY? I had asked it, worried in that earnest compassion that only a child can ever really hold for long, as if all the world felt things so tenderly, even the inanimate just wanting as badly as we did to be loved, to be heard.

WRITE ME BACK, I had written. WRITE ME BACK, IF YOU CAN.

It seems to ring in recognition, now, as I trace the entry over again.

Maybe it had. Maybe it had sought me and found me, a thousand miles upstream.

I open the mailbox all the way, trapping my pulse like a hummingbird in my wrist, and I watch as a familiar web of light spills out.

This one is stronger, brighter, fully formed and upright. She recognises me – or perhaps I recognise myself, imperceptible, gleaming from one of the many spheres of light which comprise her. The stories I gave, once, long ago.

I turn away, unable to hold it in my eyes, in my mind, the memory slipsliding, the reality dimmed by slick theft and weariness.

I turn away from the ringing hollow body dimmed by the sound of the sea, from its reaching tendrils of light, walk away until I feel the seafoam snarl around my ankles, my knees, my waist. I'm sure someone has told them this story – the wife in the attic, the cliff-jumper, the girl who wades into the water, mad with grief, mad with love, mad with the world that calls her such.

I tell myself it is not my story, but a stubborn resonance sings, like a node of light buried deep in my ribcage. It sings somewhere within me. I contain it. I am comprised of it, and others start to fly before my eyes like seabirds, white blurs against the blushing sky.

The girl echo, bound to sobbing repetition in these wild places devoid of tenderness. The huntress who lost her lover amongst the constellations. The weaver damned to forever be a creature for her justified pride. The sisters who hacked away at their own limbs to be small enough to fit. The cancer that went away like a miracle and the cancer that stayed. The girls who bear their children in terror and rage and raise them to fight, the women who bear their children like a rote chore and raise them to be silent, the girl from Nazareth who bore a saviour and lost a son, who ascended to heaven and lived a hell and never even asked for any of it.

The end. The end. The end?

Each story that speaks itself in my mind flares somewhere in me. The base of my throat, the blade of my shoulder, the tips of my fingers, my toes, each breast, and in the bowl of my womb, insistent, more and more, catching alight, there beneath muscles and sinews that now seem paper-thin, as if the real substance of me was–

A sound rises above the gentle waves' churning, and I turn back towards the shore, waist-deep in the water, seeing the flares through my skin, through the blue-green blur of the water in the fast-growing dark, and a figure is standing at the mailbox, a figure that is a web of nodes of light, a figure that is reaching…

She pulls me from the water, and we meet at the tideline. Close enough to feel the warmth radiating from her – her un-body, all this unadorned, unprotected, rushing light, this vulnerable and young communion of miniature supernovas, with no flesh to hide behind, no bounds to give the story its meaning, its reprieve, its beginning, its end.

If I touched her, she would sing all these stories back at me, sing without ceasing, adding more pinpricks of light to my being, with all these things she's witnessed, the letters to the sea, to those lost and loved and those who are somewhere, drifting still.

Luminous things, one on each side of the water, webs of witness and myth, retelling ourselves, with each pulse and sigh, we stand and see one another, and I reach out a single shaking palm to her extended one.

And then the constellation where a mouth might be flares bright in a sort of smile, and with a sound like copper bells ringing, she folds herself inwards, a brightness tightening and building, until it rushes back towards the dune, back into the mouth of the mailbox, which closed once more with a creaking sigh.

I walk a long time on the sand, pausing to observe my own body with its faint spheres glowing and bulbous beneath the skin, blurred and strange in the tide pools, but growing dimmer and dimmer. By the time night has truly fallen, I am once again a dark form, not radiant, dependent on the faint pinpricks of stars, the yet unrisen moon. All my lights have faded from view – until I stoop to pick up a shell and hear my breath catch in my throat. All but one. I stare at my left hand's centre, trace it with my other fingers. One flare lingers, a pulsing node – there in the place where our palms touched. Whose story is it, I wonder, and touch it to hear, to see, but it does not sing – it sends out a halo of silence. No images flood, no songs or hymns, no names. Only the dark coastline and the sound of my ragged breath. Whose story?

Mine, the word hisses with the reaching tide. *Mine.* I close a fist around the light, like a vow. *Mine,* I say, and I can almost hear the bells behind my voice, under my skin, what I was before the body came to me. What I will be again.

The end? I hear my own thin voice asking, waist-deep in the ocean, in the hospital bed, hands around a shaking blade, *the end?* I hear the constellation-girl echo.

No end, I promise her. The web of light under my skin sings, invisible. *No end.*

And I tell the dark a story, and it tells it back to me, and together we make for home.

WHILE I'M STILL HERE

David D. West

No one else seemed to notice when Elmer disappeared, and sadly, no one noticed when he returned.

It was the second weekend of springer season and I was sitting shoulder to shoulder along the bank with two men I had never met before. Not a word was spoken between us for nearly three hours, the sound of silence broken up only by the splashing and susurration of the river as the tide went out. We stared at our poles, waiting for a salmon to get curious enough to swallow one of our spin-n-glows whole. Mine was an ugly yellow thing, passed down to me from my father. The other guys that frequented the hole used their high-end Ugly Stiks or G. Loomis' and would pass a smirk between themselves whenever I pulled out my rod with its chipped paint and missing guides. The tip broke off at one point, reeling in a particularly violent salmon, but the pole still brought me extraordinary luck. No one else landed as many fish as I did out of that hole throughout the years.

Except maybe Elmer, back when he still showed his face around here. It was Elmer that had led me to this fishing spot, and his success here convinced me to stick around.

Dawn crested over the river just as the tide started to turn and I knew that the best fishing was only minutes away. I never reeled anything in that day, however. No one did.

The splashing of the waves was replaced by the droning of a motor and the crunch of gravel as a pickup truck pulled up somewhere above us. My unknown companions and I looked around, wondering where this newcomer was planning on casting his line. The rocky beach was small, and three poles was pushing it. A fourth pole would surely lead to tangled lines and disgruntled fishermen.

A door slammed above us. The fella to my right shifted in his camping chair, the soft canvas creaking beneath him.

Footsteps on rock.

A clunk as a chair was settled into the rocks beside me.

Elmer plopped into it.

'Mornin', Luroy.' His voice was grating, as if he hadn't used it in a while.

He didn't look at me, just stared out over the water. He certainly didn't look prepared to do any fishing; he wore a short-sleeve shirt despite the chilly morning air, the pack of snacks that sustains every fisherman during his solitary hours of meditation were either devoured already or missing, and he lacked any of the requisite gear needed to actually fish.

'Where've you been, Elmer?' The other two men watched their poles, trying to ignore us, but conditions were a little too tight to prevent eavesdropping. 'Season's been open for two weeks. I figured you'da been out here every morning.'

No response. Just that empty stare out over the water. I tried to study Elmer's face, noting how much he'd aged in the few months since I'd shared this bank with him last. He was far

64

from a young man, old enough to be my father even, but lines and bags started to reveal just how elderly he was. A hat sat on the top of his head, casting a shadow over his face and obscuring further observations.

I looked away, trying to track Elmer's gaze over the water. It was certainly hypnotic, the way the surface offered up a rippled reflection of the trees surrounding us. The rising sun flashed on the waves, blinding us intermittently as the water rolled and crashed against the rocks.

'Too crowded,' he croaked at last.

My heart sank. I carried part of the blame for the popularity of this spot. Nearly four years ago I had been driving out on some logging roads when I came across a purple truck, Elmer's truck, near the river. I peered over the bank and saw him, sitting cross-legged among the rocks with a pole in front of him, two salmon floating in a gunny sack anchored to the shore. I joined him the next day and had some of the most successful fishing of my life. A few more visits, a few friends bragged to, and the secret was out: Luroy had found himself a new honey hole. Word gets around in a small town, and soon it was a battle every morning to claim one of the three spots along the bank. That's how I explained Elmer's disappearance to myself. Fed up with fighting the flock of fishers, he ventured out in search of new country.

How wrong I would be.

'I'm sorry, Elmer. If I knew how popular this spot would become, I never woulda–'

'Don't matter now.' A wan smile crept across his face. I saw the water reflecting in his eyes, the sun shining in both. 'Found me a new place to fish.' His words confirmed my suspicions about his whereabouts, but something in his voice told me that there was more to the story. Elmer turned toward me and I recoiled at what I saw on his face.

His eyes were sunken in. His skull showed vaguely beneath his skin, which looked like it was stretched too tight across his face. He had to be sick, losing that much weight like that. His eyes had a sheen that I hadn't seen since I watched my dad kick the bucket a few years back. Elmer's eyes looked at me, but I knew he was looking right through me. He had the face of a man who knew he didn't have much time left on this Earth.

'Oh yeah? Where's that at?' I figured I had to humour him. It was my fault he ever left this bank.

'Follow me and find out. Some of the best fishing you'll ever find.' He winked at me.

Who was I to turn something like that down?

My rods bounced in the bed of my pickup as I followed Elmer's taillights down the hill. We were still out in the same neck of the woods as the last spot, but I was starting to get the sense that Elmer was taking me on a wild goose chase. We'd turned off the mainline and followed a spur a few miles back. The roads we traversed looked like they hadn't seen a human in almost a decade. But eventually the forest started to recede. The trees were spaced farther and farther apart and the blackberry bushes no longer reached out to scratch delicately at the side of our vehicles.

We turned a corner and the forest gave way to the river. The road snaked along beside it, with the water creeping up almost to the edges of the gravel. Mud caked the far side of the road, a sign that the area flooded periodically. This looked just like the spot at Stella. I felt my heart pick up a bit. Maybe Elmer really did find another honey hole, and wanted to share the beauty with me before he moved on.

Except he kept driving.

I watched the river disappear in my rearview mirror and almost slammed into the back of Elmer's truck when he screeched to a halt in the middle of the road, tires skidding in the gravel and throwing up a dust cloud.

His taillights faded as he killed the engine and stepped out of his truck. The same wan smile was still plastered across his face.

'This it?' I asked, tilting my head back toward the river.

A laugh echoed through the trees around us.

'Hope you brought your hiking boots,' Elmer said, eyes glistening.

He turned away from me, looking into the woods. 'Too rocky here. Too many snags. You see that big rock outcrop, cutting through the water? Other side of that's a beach. Nice big beach. Good fishing there. The best. Gotta hike out to it though, 'less you got a boat I don't know about.'

Elmer took a few steps forward and I saw what he was looking at: a small trail cutting through the forest. Game trail, most likely, that Elmer had adapted to his own needs.

Without another word, he started walking.

I scrambled to gather my gear, pulling my backpack over my shoulders before lifting my tackle box and pole from the bed of my truck.

'Don'tcha need your gear?'

'Already over there,' Elmer called over his shoulder without breaking stride. I hustled to catch up with him, knowing that he would leave me alone in the woods if I couldn't match his pace. I'd been there before, and I had no intention of doing that again today.

After a few dozen yards, the trail started to climb the hill. I'd seen this part of the woods before from a distance and knew that we had quite a hike ahead of us. That was one of the beauties of this part of the world. In the mountains, you could see for miles in any direction. You could watch the land rise and fall across miles, spotting where loggers had desecrated the forests, where trees had been replanted and thrived despite mankind's interventions in the natural order. Beyond the hills lay the sea, stretching out toward infinity. From the top of Brookefield, as this unit was known, you could watch the sunset over it, sending out ribbons of light to say goodnight to the world. Shadows stretched over the hills, miles long, before the sun dipped out of sight. At the top of this particular trail was a rocky outcrop. Elmer's trail had to take us right by it, but the country had looked steep.

As if reading my mind, Elmer said 'Be 'bout an hour 'fore we get to the top.'

'How long does it take to get back down the other side?' I asked between breaths. I only had 37 years under my belt, but 15 years of working on a machine hadn't been kind to my physical health. I figured Elmer would be in worse shape than me, considering his age and his apparent failing health, but the hike hardly seemed to touch him.

No answer.

Visibility dropped as the fog crept in around us. The higher we went, the thicker it got. Thin fingers of mist reached out toward us, coaxing us forward, but no matter how much we walked, we never gained any ground on them. Sounds echoed around and were bounced back to us; the crack of twigs snapping under our feet, a scruff as the toe of my boot drug against the bark of a downed log when my tired legs couldn't lift my feet high enough to clear it, the ripping of sticker bushes catching on my jacket, a jingling of my fishing lures bouncing against my pole, a few birds calling out in the trees, all the sounds you'd hear during a hike through the forest.

The rancid smell was anything but natural.

At first I thought it was the odour of fish. It started out as a mild nuisance and then grew rank once the trees started to disperse around us. We had to be near the top of the hill. I wrinkled my nose, wishing for a breath of fresh air, but the stench was pervasive.

'I don't know how much more I can take of this, Elmer.' My lungs screamed from the hike and breathing in the putrid stench offered no respite. Elmer's pace only added to the difficulties. My hair glued to my forehead with sweat. 'Something die around here?'

'Up 'round the ways a little, yeah.' He offered no further explanation.

The smell intensified with each step, but the fog started lifting. We crested the top of the hill and were suddenly above the fog. Looking behind me, I saw nothing but trees reaching through the blanket of mist, a million fingers stretching to the clouds. In front of me, the hill sloped down to meet a thin strip of beach. A few cargo ships made their way up the river, pushing water against the tide. The path forked at our feet. To the right, the knob stood towering over the river and forest.

'Need to make a pitstop thata way, grab my gear. Keep it stashed up here so I don't have to pack it both ways.' His voice wavered as he talked. I couldn't tell if it was trepidation or anticipation.

I followed Elmer as he turned down the path leading to the knob. The ground was bare, stamped flat by what seemed like steady usage. Elmer picked up his pace, almost sprinting toward the base of the knob. My knees ached but still I followed, not wanting to be abandoned up here.

We circled the knob. The far side, away from the river, was a sheer rock face. Beneath it, a stone valley. Boulders as big as Elmer's pickup littered the area. Trees lined the edge of the valley, and through it I could see an assortment of colours.

Tents?

The place was set up almost like an amphitheatre, with the rock bluff the main attraction.

I stopped. Elmer, as if sensing my hesitation, paused as well. He turned toward me, face sombre.

The wind picked up, pushing me into the arena. I wanted to turn and run, to get back to my pickup and just find a new place to fish, a place where I would never run into Elmer again.

'Don't you see it, Luroy?' He gestured over his shoulder to the stone wall. Trees sprouted from the earth above it. Roots dangled in the air, snaking their way down the sheer face. A living crown. 'That's God. He's been hiding up here for years, waiting for us to find Him. To worship Him.'

I glanced at the knob. There were indentations here and there, cracks running horizontally at random intervals, but nothing that made me think that this natural formation was anything divine.

'You've been watching *The Blue Lagoon* a little too much, Elmer.' I took a step backward. 'Come on, let's get out of here. Get down to the beach before the tide changes.'

I felt a hand on my shoulder, clamping down too tight. I tried to spin, face whatever was grabbing me, but the grip was too tight.

Behind Elmer, people emerged from the woods. Some of them wore clothes, but the majority were naked. They crawled out of tents, pushed through bushes, appeared out of nothingness. Some filed toward the base of the knob while others made their way over to where Elmer and I stood. Each carried something long and silver in their hands.

'You need to meet Him.' Elmer's voice wasn't much more than a whisper. Desperation saturated his eyes.

As the people moved closer I could see what they were carrying.

Fish.

Some salmon, some steelhead. The occasional sturgeon was carted by, needing two people to carry its massive length. One person went by with two rainbow trout in their hands, no doubt caught from one of the many small lakes that dotted the landscape. They assembled at the base of the cliff, and raised the fish above their heads.

The world was silent. The rotten smell overpowering. I squinted my eyes, water forming at the edges. One by one, the congregation threw their fish at the bluff. The fish plopped and slapped against the rocks, leaving behind scales and slime as they bounced into a pile at the base of the bluff. The mound grew as the crowd dispersed, free from their offerings. They didn't retreat into the woods, but gave enough breathing room to the cliffs they were worshipping.

As if they were waiting for their God to answer, to smile down on them in benevolence.

A scream cut through the air. On the other side of the arena, a woman was being pushed toward the knob. The person behind me shoved me in turn, and I knew the woman was in the same situation I found myself in. Did she get lured here with the promise of the world's best fishing, or did something else entice her to the top of the mountain? I dug my heels into the ground, but there was nothing to give me purchase. My shoes skittered across the stone as I leaned back, watching wide-eyed at what was unfurling before me.

Two boulders lay side by side at the base of the knob, where the rock face met the ground at a perfect 90-degree angle. The top of each boulder had been smashed and chipped until they were nearly flat, two slabs before the stone god above. They were stained a dark red colour. The pile of fish sat neatly between the two slabs, stinking to the high heavens. People gathered around and kneeled before the slabs, never taking their eyes off the face of the cliff.

Humming broke out among the congregation, a low guttural sound, as I was pushed closer and closer to the two slabs. Elmer moved to the foot of one slab, turned to face the crowd.

The woman who had screamed was thrown on top of her slab, where a dozen hands reached up to hold her in place. She struggled against them, screaming louder than ever, but there were too many people restraining her.

Another pair of hands pressed against my back, urging me forward.

I was next.

'Elmer!' I screamed. He never looked at me, only stared down at his people.

More hands. Ripping my pole away from me, lifting my feet, guiding me toward my own slab. I was thrown down and I felt all the air leave my lungs. Just as well, I thought. Better to be breathless than suffer that fishy smell again.

Hands grabbed my wrists, ankles, neck, everything they could reach. It was as if the hands were coming straight from the boulder, like the earth itself was trying to welcome me back to the soil I would one day return to.

The sun sank toward the horizon. Night would fall soon. It slid behind the knob and the crown of trees erupted in fire. Shadows danced over the crowd of people, who cheered.

The mountain teemed with life.

I watched as the rock bluff morphed, changed, produced a face.

Two eyes stared down at me, deep, dark pits of hatred.

A disapproving frown crested below the eyes. In a manic moment, I tried to think back to whatever sin brought me here, what I had to confess before this ancient lord of the earth, but my mind drew a blank.

Fish.

That was the only thing I could think of.

The smell prevented my thoughts from landing on anything else. Was it because I led others to Elmer's secret spot, all those years ago? Had I broken the sacred bond of a fisherman, to respond with a simple 'No-Tell-um Creek' when asked where I caught my limit?

The face stared down at me, silently judging. The crowd fell silent, staring up at the face of their god.

I blinked tears out of my eyes.

'I'm sorry, Elmer. I'm sorry I told anyone about that spot. If I woulda known so many people would take it over, I never woulda followed you that day.'

A great shushing from the crowd. I was interrupting something.

I watched the face of God.

But the face of God really was nothing more than a rock outcropping. Where I thought I saw eyes was really just shadows dancing around the dimples and imperfections of the bluff. The frown was nothing more than a fracture, cut into the rock from some primordial earthquake. There were nearly a hundred people gathered here this evening. How had all of them been deceived by a trick of the light?

It sure was convincing though. One second I saw God staring down at me, ready to cast His judgment through the hands of this piscine congregation. Then the light would shift as the sun crawled across the sky and the face would disappear. It happened a few times in the minute we all watched the bluff together.

Were they waiting for confirmation on His existence as well?

'It's just a rock!' I yelled. I screamed it as loud as I could, and I had to scream to be heard over the woman next to me. 'It's just a–'

A hand clamped down over my mouth, sealing the words.

Another hand grabbed me by the temple and forced my head to the left, to watch the woman laying on the other slab.

A figure stalked toward her, some hooded member of the congregation (or perhaps the leader) who was too good to get down on their knees before their god. They stood between Elmer and the woman's captor, who still stood at the foot of their slab. Elmer and the other captor were two shining stars tonight, the faithful who had offered up tonight's sacrifices.

The hooded figure pulled a knife from behind their back and offered it to the woman. She stepped up to the slab and the captive woman's screams were silenced by the realisation of what was about to happen to her.

The knife sliced through the air, a deafening sound in the silence, and sunk into the woman's stomach. Dozens of hands reached into the open wound, pulling forth entrails and holding them aloft to the god of stone. The leader of the group reached into the mass of frenzied hands, grabbed the woman's heart, and threw it at the bluff. It landed in the centre of the scales that now decorated the cliff before landing on top of the pile of fish like a cherry on the world's worst sundae.

A raven cawed somewhere in the distance.

A cargo ship blasted its fog horn.

The sun dipped even further behind the knob and the shadowy face shifted again. A look of pleasure, of gratitude, spread across the rock.

One offering out of the way, every eye trained on me. The hooded figure took the knife from the woman and offered it to Elmer.

I got a glimpse of the person underneath the cloak, just for a second.

Looking back, I could have sworn they had a fish's head, that they were adding to the putrid smell.

Elmer took the knife and took a step toward me.

The sun sank ever lower, finally dipped over the horizon, and the shadowy rock face disappeared.

A sigh washed through the crowd. Hands relaxed and I had my body to myself again, for the time being.

'And so He is satisfied with our offering. Sorry to have to put you through all that, Luroy. You came away lucky, though, dont'cha think?'

I glanced over to the slab next to me, at the ruined remains of the woman there.

The congregation dispersed as fast as it had formed. Satisfied with whatever blessing they'd received from their lord, they filed back into the woods and into their tents. Elmer stayed behind though, with my fishing gear in a pile behind him. He reached down and picked up my father's pole.

Handed it to me.

I wanted to run, but what good would it do? I could feel hundreds of eyes on me, watching through the trees. They would never let me leave this place alive after what I'd witnessed.

He led me away from the arena. When we reached the fork in the path that would take me back home, we went the other way, toward the beach waiting below. The sun was below the horizon now and the sky exploded with colours. Reds and violets and scarlets lit up the world, to match the entrails that had been ripped out of a woman not ten feet from me.

The beach was pristine. The waves came in and washed away evidence of any interlopers every six hours, leaving a blank canvas behind.

Elmer handed me my gear and took a seat in the sand. The sound of the water coming in on itself, the sand shifting underneath it, was hypnotic. I watched the sky darken over the calm water. I saw my reflection on that ever shifting mirror and barely recognised myself. My face was white against the night sky.

I cast my pole out, my line whizzing through the night air. I fell to the ground next to Elmer and we spent some time looking out over the water.

'How long do I have?'

Elmer made a clicking sound next to me.

'Hard telling. He's pretty unreliable. Sometimes He demands it three times a day. That gets pretty rough on us. Sometimes He'll go a week before he needs to be satiated. Depends on the weather mostly.'

I nodded my head. 'And no chance you'll let me go? Let me sneak back through the woods on my own, say I tricked you somehow?'

'No chance. Not while He's still up there.'

Neither of us said much of anything after that.

I could see the congregation guarding us, making sure I didn't leave the beach. They waited for Elmer and me too reel in the next offering, for their God to want that offering, to lay me down on that slab and gut me like a–

Maybe. Maybe they would gut me. Or maybe I could join them? Pretend to play their game. Throw some fish of my own while chanting whatever nonsense rippled through the crowd, let some other poor bastard lay their life down. I could even offer to go find someone, lead them up to the mountain.

All as a ruse. Of course. I would escape the first chance I got. Wouldn't I?

I'd have some time to think on it. To make a plan.

In the meantime, Elmer and I never left the beach.

And he was right, you know.

It really was some of the best fishing I'd ever had.

TO ALL THOSE WHO EXIST IN THE UNIVERSE

Jamie Perrault

The echoes of *Voyager's* transmission play crisp and clean over the radio that has been tuned to receive them for the last few weeks.

'Shalom.' Coda whispers along with the string of greetings again, their lips forming each word just a moment ahead of the radio. 'Hola y saludos a todos.'

The door to the observatory opens, and Hera stalks in. A moment later she drops into the seat next to Coda, sipping at something that smells more like rubber than anything potable should. 'Anything changed?'

Coda shakes their head. 'The object is still transmitting *Voyager*'s record. Still moving steadily forward. Our new neighbours are just a little past Mars now. They should be here in a week, barring trajectory changes.'

Hera blows on her coffee. 'Anyone decided what we're going to do yet?'

Coda shrugs. 'That's above my pay grade now.'

'Pay grade.' Hera rolls her eyes. 'You're so old-fashioned.'

Coda doesn't respond. They're thirty-five years older than Hera; they lived through the societal collapses and rippling changes in alliances that reshaped the world, whereas she was born into the aftermath.

Sighing – whether in frustration at not getting a response from Coda or irritation that nobody has come up with a plan yet, Coda can't even guess – Hera looks over Coda's data. 'I wish it would send us something new. Something that's not just our own words.'

'If it's sending something new, it's probably in those data packets we can't read.' Coda stretches, mouthing the Japanese question *how are you* along with the transmission.

'Nope.' Hera grimaces. 'Intel sent out a package about two hours ago saying those are just the same sounds as the radio transmission. Maybe whoever's out there wants to make sure we're getting the message?'

'Maybe.' Coda gives their head another shake, forcing themself to stop echoing the aliens who are spouting Earth's words back at them. 'We'll see soon enough. If you're all set here, I'll–'

Half the alarms on the dashboard go off, flashing lights and cyclical pulses of sound that indicate something has drastically changed.

Hera very carefully sets her cup down before pointing at the screen that shows the relative position of all astronomical bodies currently under investigation. 'Coda, is that– did it just–'

Coda gives themself a moment to run their tongue over their lip before nodding. 'It did. Call upstairs, Hera. Our guests aren't going to be here next week. They're going to be here in about five minutes.'

Six nation-states fire at the alien vessel.

It has to be an alien vessel at this point. There had still been some people holding out, wondering if perhaps *Voyager*'s data had been placed on an inert astrological body and then flung back into the solar system by unknown forces. The object had followed a fairly straight trajectory, after all, and maintained a consistent course after being spotted in the vicinity of Saturn's orbit.

Had that consistency been intended to give them peace of mind? Or had it been something else, the vessel searching for signs that humanity had advanced beyond the dreams installed on *Voyager* in the two hundred years since it was sent out into the ether?

Coda can't help a bitter smile at the thought. Humanity has survived, of course; that's something people are always good at. There's enough stubbornness, enough love, enough ability to play fairly with others in *enough* people that humanity always survives.

But it hasn't thrived. The world hasn't thrived around them. The dreams of the past have been swallowed by the realities of a future that could be worse – Coda knows it could be so much worse. The economic and agricultural collapse could have been worse. The fascists could have fully taken power, making it so Coda faced torment for the colour of their skin or their gender or their disinterest in romance or the way they worship with the moon or the way their father wears a Sikh turban to show his faith.

But it should be so much better. Humanity had so many opportunities, so many *options*, and because of the greed and hatred and fear of a few, those chances kept slipping through everyone's collective fingers.

As this opportunity may soon be gone, because surely being greeted with missile fire was not what these entities expected after spending weeks broadcasting Earth's supposedly-peaceful messages back to them.

Coda doesn't watch the broadcasts that show the carnage. They know what missile strikes look like. Instead they stand outside the observatory staring up at the stars – the stars that have always called to them, enticed them, enriched them.

If death is coming, Coda wants to face it here. Let whatever alien weapons there are obliterate them where they stand. Let the stars be covered by plant-destroying ash while they watch.

If the world is going to burn, let the last thing Coda sees be the promise of a broader universe.

Nothing happens, though. For ten… twenty… sixty minutes after retaliation should have happened, there's no sign of death in the night sky.

Pulling their tablet from their pocket, Coda scrolls to the news feed. The world is a big place, after all. If the end started somewhere else, they may need to stand here a little bit longer in order to see it.

The alien vessel hasn't attacked, though. It hasn't done anything other than move.

Move at impossible speeds, dodging left and right and up and down and forward and backward, skipping just above Earth's atmosphere as missiles either detonate or continue uselessly into space.

There will likely be tidal effects from that dancing – a kilometre-long vessel moving like that will surely have *some* impact – but it isn't doing anything other than protecting itself.

Drawing in a long breath – feeling the cool green scents of growing things fill their nostrils – Coda turns and marches back into the observatory.

The alien vessel came with greetings, and it hasn't attacked despite ample provocation.

If there's a chance to make this encounter – this wondrous, perfect, dreamt-of encounter – work out in Earth's favour, Coda wants to be a part of it.

Coda is the oldest astronaut allowed on the mission.

There's a high probability of failure. The alien vessel is enormous and far more manoeuvrable than anything the fragments of NASA and her integrated space programs have salvaged or built over the last four decades. Coda and their three younger companions could find themselves unable to get close to the great ship, instead aiming for an emergency landing in whatever large body of water they can find.

Coda hears all about this possibility for the sixty-eighth time as Jeb tries to convince them that going on the mission is a terrible idea.

'Jeb.' Coda cuts into the Observer leader's carefully constructed argument. 'We're heading up in four hours. You don't have time to replace me.'

'You aren't replaceable. That's the problem.' Jeb's jaw sets a little tighter.

'I am.' Jeb is proof of that. Coda made sure Jeb could do everything that was needed before Coda handed him the observatory on a silver platter. 'I've been interviewed forward and backward on everything I remember about the transition periods I lived through. I've recorded all my astronomical knowledge, passing it on to younger and smarter people. I don't know any languages that others here don't.'

'But you do know six of them, which is two more than anyone else on the team right now.' Jeb crosses his arms in front of his chest, scowling. The stubborn determination and loyalty that drove Coda to choose him in the first place are less appealing now.

'But I don't know anything *unique*. Give the kids here a little more time, and I bet there'll be a polyglot to blow me out of the water. I'm sure of it.' Reaching out to place a hand on Jeb's shoulder, Coda holds eye contact for long enough to see Jeb's defences start to crumble before giving their friend's shoulder a squeeze. 'I need to do this, Jeb. I don't have anything more to offer here. I've given more than my all. I'm *tired*. Let me see the stars before I'm done.'

Jeb sighs, all the muscles in his shoulders seeming to relax at once. 'I don't suppose I could talk you into taking back this job? Handling whatever this first-contact ends up being in my place?'

'Nope. I'm all out of patience to give to people acting like idiots.' Coda grins.

'Going up into space isn't going to help that.' Jeb's humour drops away, the tension already creeping back into his posture. 'The people who shot at the ship aren't just going to sit idly by. There's a good chance you'll be fighting up there, and if you do happen to make contact with any aliens, you might be having to argue with some of our fellow humans about what should be done with said aliens.'

'But I'll have made contact with alien life.' Coda shrugs, unable to stop the smile that steals across their face. If they die trying something like that… they know for a fact far worse fates have claimed far better people. 'Can I go finish getting ready?'

Jeb waves a hand. 'Go on, then. Live some dreams for all of us.'

Coda doesn't think they'll be doing *that* – doesn't know if they still have dreams that are worth living – but they know they need to be heading up into the stars.

After a life spent scrabbling to survive without sacrificing every dream their child-self ever had, feeling like this is the only path they can possibly take is beautifully freeing.

'I don't think this is a good idea.' San's voice shakes, their hands tight against their safety restraints. 'Look at that thing. Those are tentacles. That's a kilometre-long tentacle beast.'

'And we're in a glorified flying car.' It's not, really – it's far beyond what the original billionaires could have dreamed of, designed for better manoeuvrability in space as well as to survive multiple re-entry attempts. But it was built on the bones of those selfish endeavours, and Coda can never forget that – will never let others forget it. 'Whoever these people are, they've been saying hello just like we asked the universe to. It's rude of humanity to have second thoughts about it now.'

'They have a giant *tentacle ship*.' San turns their wide, wondering eyes on Coda.

Coda shrugs. 'Great way to arrange propulsion in three dimensions.'

'Does anyone have a suggestion for approaching the kilometre-long flying tentacle beast?' Raquel's voice is barely more than a whisper, but it fills the small cockpit.

'I'll keep broadcasting the *Voyager* record.' San's fingers glance across the communication's array, though they don't change anything.

'No.' Coda studies the ship – the impossible, beautiful, horrifying glory of it. 'No, that's not what we do. If we'd been prepared, we would have made another record with a different set of connected messages, but since we didn't… let me broadcast.'

San eyes Coda, their young, unlined face giving away their wariness. 'What are you intending to do?'

'Ask politely for a docking location.' Coda smiles. 'If it works, I'll buy us all lunch in whatever weird alien snack bars we can find.'

'That should not have worked.' Raquel shivers.

They've parked the rover in the strange space that rippled open on the side of the vessel after Coda's third repetition of a request for docking.

'What do we do now?' Billi speaks for the first time since they launched, his voice soft and hesitant. 'Do we go out there? I can't see anything but more of that dark… stuff. Building material?'

Coda somehow expected Billi to say *skin*, and is glad he didn't. 'Either that or we turn around and fly right back out.'

None of them are willing to do that, of course. They've come too far; they've sunk too much into this already. Besides, if they're not the first contact point, who's to say it won't be someone worse?

Except… that's not why Coda wants to be here. Coda wants to be here because there is a *ship*, a great enormous vessel, and it came saying *their own words* back to them. It came from the dark, and has done wondrous things, and despite humanity being just as terrible and unpredictable as ever, it hasn't run.

Checking their helmet and gloves, Coda reaches for the hatch. 'I'm going out. Everyone else is welcome to do as they'd like.'

There's no more debate, no more hesitation. With a thick rustling sound, everyone finishes checking the seals on their suits before declaring themselves ready.

Heart feeling too big for their chest, Coda opens the hatch, letting themself into the airlock. They'll have to exit one at a time, and Coda wants to be first.

It doesn't take long for the hatch to cycle. A few determined twists of their hands, and Coda is able to float down – no, to *fall down*.

There shouldn't be gravity here, not where they are in relation to Earth, but Coda's legs are drawn inexorably towards the ground.

It feels… solid. Believable. Like a real ship's floor, certain and sturdy. Only the appearance is wrong, a deep glistening black that turns to iridescent rainbows in the light from Coda's suit.

Two minutes must have passed, because San comes tumbling out of the airlock and down to stand at Coda's side. '*Now* what are you planning?' they demand.

Coda considers, and then says with a sharp grin, 'We're continuing on.'

The answers to who these aliens are and what they want is somewhere in here. Coda just needs the right question, and a way to understand what's said back.

'This is incredible.' Raquel breathes out the words, only the headsets in their helmets allowing Coda to hear her.

It took their crew about twenty minutes to find the exit from the landing area – twenty minutes in which Billi and San alternated paranoid fantasies about how they're in the stomach of the monster, having delivered themselves for digestion.

Once through the little airlock they found, though, the world they walked into exceeded words.

'It's all alive.' San reaches out, their gloved hand running over a plant that creeps along the iridescent wall. The leaves vibrate at their touch, but they don't pull away.

Nothing pulls away from them. Not the plants, not the little scaled creatures that are skittering and scurrying between the green and purple growing things, not the creatures that could be insects or could be birds or could be something else entirely.

Nothing is afraid of them, and some part of Coda screams that everything *should be*. Screams that there is no safety to be had for them or their crew here, in this place where nothing knows that humanity is to be respected.

Screams that there is no safety to be had for these incredible, impossible aliens if they do not know that humans are to be feared above all other creatures.

'We should take samples and go back already.' Billi's voice hasn't risen above a whisper still. 'This is beyond us. This is beyond the Observers. Maybe this will be a chance for us to actually make some proper alliances again, to try to get humanity unified behind a common cause.'

'We need to see more.' Coda keeps their voice neat and even, not allowing any of the strain or fear or wonder they feel to infect their tone. A scientist must be rational, after all, even if what they're seeing is not.

There are too many turns and branches in the vessel to keep track of without better equipment. Coda contents themself with the main path, choosing always the biggest of the tunnels to continue through. White-blue light glows down from the ceiling, giving everything a strange, surreal look.

Something large steps out of a side tunnel.

Coda freezes, and the sound of the crew moving behind and beside them subsides, fading away to almost nothing as they all realise they're being watched.

Cat, Coda's mind tries to say. Except it very clearly isn't a cat. It has two eyes, certainly, and they are slit-pupiled. But it has six legs, and eight tails distributed between the legs and along the dorsal ridge. In lieu of fur it has green tendrils that float in a soft corona around it, making it impossible to judge the thing's size beyond *big*. Almost as tall as Coda, and possibly longer.

Stepping forward, Coda raises a hand and sets their helmet to project sound. 'Silim-ma he-me-en.' Their tongue stumbles on the old Sumerian words, but since they're the first greeting on the *Voyager* record it feels appropriate. 'Welcome, traveller.'

The not-cat studies their crew, not flinching, not approaching beyond the confines of the tunnel it came from. Then it bows, front legs sliding forward so that the head drops almost to the floor. Opening its mouth, the alien begins making sounds. They're far more mangled than Coda's attempt at Sumerian, but Coda recognises them. They've listened to them often enough over the last few weeks. 'Hoitines pot'este chairete.'

Greetings to you, whoever you are.

The alien studies each of them in turn, yellow-blue eyes in a green face, and then turns to walk back the way it came.

Coda doesn't hesitate to follow.

San grabs Coda's shoulder, their voice over the comm link an octave higher than usual. 'Coda, please, be careful.'

Coda considers. 'You three be careful. We'll need someone to go home, to tell what we've found.'

They don't say more than that. What is there to say?

How can they condense a lifetime's worth of being careful into a story that these young ones will understand? Careful is how humanity survived – how *civilisation* survived. Careful is how Coda survived, and how they helped make the world that their crewmates will inherit – a world that is broken, but not beyond salvation.

Coda doesn't want to be careful now. They want to see what it is that this creature offers. They want to drown themselves in the wonder that surrounds them, and see if they will be allowed to float instead of sink.

They follow the creature, pulling free of San's hand with gentle implacability.

They hear the sound of the others following; they hear the sound of the others debating, their voices filling Coda's helmet, but that doesn't matter now.

The cat-creature doesn't run. It just walks, and there is something in the way it moves that shivers through Coda's brain with an acute awareness that it is *not from here*.

But it is recognisably alive, as is everything else on this ship, and that means they are all siblings in the vast, quiet universe.

The cat-creature finally comes to a halt in front of a glowing golden waterfall. The liquid falls from the ceiling and disappears into the floor, a luminescent sheet that flows just a little too slowly to be water.

Coda steps up beside the cat-creature, looking from it to the glowing waterfall.

With deliberate steps, the alien immerses its face in the waterfall. Eyes closed, it bathes in the liquid.

Everything around them starts to shiver, and the vibrations form words that are familiar to Coda – one of the languages of their home.

One of the languages of *Voyager*.

One of the pleas a younger, harsher, still-hopeful humanity sent out into the dark and the quiet.

Aao ji, jee aya nu.

Welcome home; it is a pleasure to have you.

'Coda–' Raquel's voice breaks through the vibrations, stopping Coda's first step into the golden flow from completing. 'Are you really going to do this?'

Coda turns, hands rising to their helmet. 'If it goes badly, tell Jeb it was just an accident.'

Then their helmet is off, and alien air touches their face. It's cooler than Coda expected, and moister. It smells of growing things – not quite the same as Earth's smell, but Coda isn't sure if that's because so much of Earth smells of human encroachment now or because there is something impossibly alien here.

Keeping their eyes on their crewmates – all still properly suited, their expressions impossible to make out through their helmets – Coda walks backward into the golden waterfall.

The liquid coats their hair, creates a film against their skin, seeps into their ears and eyes and mouth. It doesn't hurt, but Coda shivers anyway, waiting for what comes next.

For one minute, then two, nothing happens. They start to feel foolish standing in the waterfall, their suit filled with liquid, their skin sticking awkwardly to the fabric. They raise a hand to wave sheepishly at their companions.

And something goes *snap* deep in the recesses of their body.

It's like a lightning strike to the chest; like the touch of fire to their soul. It's the deepest meditation and the strongest intoxication, and Coda both experiences it and watches it from afar.

Welcome, traveller.

The words are a part of their body. They are something that Coda speaks and something that is spoken to them and something that is spoken *through* them.

Turning their eyes seems to take an enormous effort, but they manage to look down at the cat-creature. It closes its eyes, the expression almost like the affectionate eye-squeeze a cat at home would have done.

Because it is *trying* to be like a cat at home, to speak so that Coda will understand.

We do not mean any harm.

The one who speaks isn't the cat. The one who speaks is the *ship*; is the home; is the world that contains all those who have given themselves to it.

You called to us. Softly, as a tired child would, but you called.

The voices from the *Voyager* record sing in Coda's heart, and they speak them aloud, sending them rippling through the shared ecosystem of the ship-world.

Raquel, San, and Billi have all gathered together, forming a protective triangle. They begin backing slowly down the corridor.

They don't see the others coming.

The others weren't supposed to come here. Each group of travellers was to have their own guide, their own chance to explain.

These two have been carving a path through the ship, though, firing weapons indiscriminately, and that doesn't change when the figures they shoot at are clearly human.

Billi falls, and though blood doesn't erupt from the puncture in his suit, Coda and the cat can smell it.

Stop!

The thought is a desperate shout, and everything in the vicinity responds to it. One moment the cat is at Coda's side; the next it is slashing and slicing at the ones who attacked.

One moment the plants are content to crawl their slow way along the vessel walls; the next they are moving to trap limbs, to prevent motion.

Four more shots are fired, but none manage to puncture vital organs. The guns clatter to the floor, and Coda reaches down to pick one of them up.

Where are these people from?

The ship wants to know, but Code knows it doesn't matter. They're human, as Coda is human. They came in a ship likely very similar to the one Coda rode in, and they brought with them the death and destruction that is always, always at humanity's fingertips.

While Coda holds the gun, Raquel and San work on Billi. Opening his suit releases the blood that had been contained, and Coda doesn't need to hear Raquel's cry to know how it will sound – to know how desperate the situation is.

What do you want, traveller?

If the ship is perturbed by what happened, it doesn't show in the voice that fills Coda's entire being.

I want this to stop. Coda tries and fails to crush the gun.

I cannot control your people. The ship wouldn't even if it could. Those who come to the ship come willingly. Those who wish to leave are free to do so. *Do you think you are worth welcoming, or should we send you all home again?*

Are they worth welcoming? Such an impossible question. Coda closes their eyes, sinking into the sensations of the ship.

There are six other groups of people on the vessel already. Eight groups of people in total who reached for the stars as soon as it seemed they were reachable.

One of those groups is attempting to dig up plants and capture animals.

Another is planting bombs, and Coda makes sure the ship understands the danger before they open their eyes and look down at the gun again.

Allowing the weapon to drop the deck, Coda moves to Billi's side and grabs him under both arms. Raquel's helmet is off, and she looks up at Coda, tear-streaked expression filled with terror. 'What are you doing?'

Coda speaks six languages, but all they can manage to do is nod towards the waterfall, Billi's arm held tight.

Drawing in a deep breath, Raquel nods and lifts Billi's other arm. Together they drag his limp form towards the liquid.

'Help him.' Coda doesn't know what language they whisper the words in as they settle Billi's unconscious form into the shimmering liquid. 'Help him if you can. The rest of us... we're trying. We're trying so hard, but there's so many of our siblings who are afraid, and a few who are just... just...'

Damaging. Destructive.

Coda's whole body flinches, the concepts that those words represent rocking through their body, their memories, their dreams. 'I don't know if we're worth anything, but so many of us want to see the stars. So many of us want to welcome our star-siblings. Does that make up for how badly we've failed our own planet? For how we've failed our own people?'

You didn't hold the weapon, you know. The words are a gentle glowing cradle that holds Coda's body.

I didn't. I just didn't take it away, or figure out how to stop all the people who want them. Not for lack of trying, but Coda also knows they could have tried harder. If they didn't need to sleep, if they didn't need to rest, if they'd been willing to keep leading, to keep scrabbling with the already-raw and bloody fingers of their determination–

Billi's eyes open, and he gasps, his body arching as he reaches towards his wound and Coda's hand at the same time.

His eyes shine gold, the same colour as the waterfall he's lying in. Coda wonders briefly if their eyes glow now, too.

You want your companion to live. You came in peace and wonder and reverence. The whole ship shudders around them, a shiver to match Coda's as their fingers clasp Billi's.

You come with death and destruction, wanting nothing more than to erase everything you see as not-you. Coda's vision blanks out, replaced by vibration-temperature-scent that indicates threats.

What should we do with your people, Coda? The question is all-consuming, a wash of sensation that Coda can't even name.

So they give the same answer they've given every time they ask the question of themself. *Give us a chance. Give us just one more chance to prove that there's enough about us to make salvation worthwhile.*

Billi's eyes flare bright, and he speaks in Punjabi, a language he doesn't know. 'I think that gives us more than enough to work with.'

When Raquel's fingers tentatively touch Coda's shoulder, Coda turns to smile up at her. Licking their lips, they fumble for a language they share. 'I don't know if it's all going to be all right, but I think we've still got a chance.'

It's the last thing that Coda says for a little while, the world dissolving into golden light and more data inputs than their human mind can possibly hope to process, but it's really all that needs to be said.

'You're different.'

Coda smiles at Jeb. 'Is it the glowing eyes that give it away?'

Jeb laughs. 'They're certainly something, but it's more… you're *here* in a way that you haven't been in a long time. Not for years.'

Coda nods, though being *here* is relative right now. They are always aware of *there* – of the great ship that currently orbits Earth, waiting to see who will come aboard. 'Thank you. For giving me the opportunity to try this. It… reminds me that there are times I'm happy, with myself and with this world.'

'I'm glad.' Jeb's expression melts between emotions, too many and too complicated for Coda to keep up with. Joy, sorrow, loss, acceptance – they're all there.

Just one complicated human among many.

One *friend*.

Jeb's expression settles on worried. 'You're offering everyone a place on the ship?'

Coda shrugs. 'Those who want it. Those who will work. But this is still our world, and we owe it a great debt. It should still be ours. Or– *we* should still be a part of *it*.'

'Yeah?' Jeb pauses, his foot scuffing back and forth through the dirt. 'Glad to hear you feel that way, because *I* won't leave.'

Coda smiles, nodding in understanding. 'Good. Earth can still be beautiful.'

Jeb exhales, returning Coda's smile. 'And the people of Earth?'

'Those, too.' When they're not trying to kill each other; when they're not trying to kill everything that *isn't* human; when they're diving headfirst into the great chaos that is reality rather than trying to bend the universe to fit into narrow boxes...

Coda would have found it easier to give up a long time ago if people couldn't be so damn wonderful when they're not being terrible. Slinging an arm around Jeb's shoulders, they gesture back towards the observatory that is currently the centre of diplomatic negotiations. 'Let's see how much sense we can talk into everyone, all right?'

Jeb nods. 'I'm down for some nonsense, too, as long as it moves things forward peacefully.'

Coda laughs, and walks forward with their friend, into a future that is just as uncertain and wondrous and terrifying as ever.

YOU'LL BE GONE
BY MORNING

Courtney Smyth

As sure as the sun rises, Irish people love a funeral.

Maybe it's the years of pain and loss in our richly tumultuous past; some latent grief that needs intergenerational purging. Maybe it's that we're a nation of poets and writers, musicians and dancers, dreamers and believers, anchoring ourselves to the Earth with the surety of a bereavement. And so it's fair to also say we love a wake. We love to remember. We love to clamour to deliver the morbid gossip – *did you hear who died* – and decide if we should attend the mass, pop out to a funeral home of an evening, shake the hands of the mourners and tell them *I'm sorry for your loss.* We remember the dead well – even if we didn't know them alive. In a nation of storytellers, perhaps no one ever dies if even one person remembers.

Maybe that's why we don't ask what happens when you pass. Even the ones who don't believe in a god or a heaven will never be caught dead – no pun intended – allowing themselves to ponder this question seriously. Not over reminiscent pints in the local, or even when pouring over the obituaries in the papers with ink-stained fingers and a rasher sandwich in one hand on a Sunday morning. Not in hospital beds, in sickness, in old age, in fear, in sadness, we don't allow ourselves to ask the question. As sure as we love a wake, we love to believe we'll never have to know.

Brona was just a girl when she learned wicker baskets weren't the best choice for liquids, even if they're lined – though it's also important to note that she didn't *choose* to learn this. She didn't elect to find the baskets; she didn't wish for their contents. None of them ever did. If a basket found its way to you, well. You were chosen and that was that. No amount of hiding or refusing or wanting to believe in anything else would change the facts of it. It's what you chose after that. That's the bit you could control.

Of course Brona fought it, for a time. It didn't stop the wicker baskets appearing overnight, when she was a girl – though perhaps not quite a girl at 18, but young enough for older women to say *maith an cailín* when she paid for stuff in the local shop, for her to be referred to as the nice youngwan, girleen; reminders of her youth, reminders not to ask where you go when you pass because she had so much life ahead of her.

It all started with a beat, as many things did. Though maybe it started before that. Brona had laid her pet bird to rest just three nights prior; he had fallen from his wooden perch with a final shout and landed spread-winged at the bottom of his cage. Brona choked on her tears as she rearranged his feathers and placed him in a wood box that had once housed a semi-decent red wine, brought it outside, covered it with cloth and copper salt and set it alight. Her face bathed in flickering shadows as the moon rose and the salt burned blue-green, the once-colour of his feathers. She buried the ashes in the soil beneath the great oak tree at the end of her road, carefully replacing the sod she'd trowelled out so the neighbours didn't pitch a fit about leaving scraps for the foxes to forage, even if there were no scraps to be found. It was a sacred place for him, a sacred place for her. Brona didn't want to have to prove anything about it, so she moved in secret. Only the moon saw.

Maybe she called the baskets to her, all things considered. The earth, the fire, the moon and the little extinguished life. Her tears and her anguish, a maelstrom of opportunity for something to happen. She'd wonder about it for years to come.

Once he was buried, she lay in her bed for three days, the sadness too much to bear. He had been her companion. *He was just a bird*, her family said. Her friends, returning from another funeral, made sure to point out how *some people had it worse*. That was another favourite fall-back in remembering: remember, but not too much. Nobody is alone in their misery when there's greater misery to be had. Brona had witnessed misery with them, trod the boards of creaky funeral homes, stood and said the phrases in dusty churches choked with incense, watched hearses line up and be brought on to crematoriums and cemeteries with great towers watching over those lain to rest. The bird was her friend. Her companion. The first time she'd realised *I'm sorry for your loss* was not enough, though it was hardly said at all.

It was in her bed at the close of the third day that she heard the beat for the first time. At first, she thought it was distant hammering, building work out on the main road. Then she thought it was a clock with a broken mechanism, beating out a heavy, steady *thump thump thump thump*. She got out of her bed and searched around her room, turning the lights on, squinting in the imposing flare as her eyes adjusted in her quest for the source of the noise. It didn't take long to find it. A lidded wicker basket, lined in white cotton, tucked underneath her bed. Magenta liquid soaked into the burnt-pine orange of her floorboards. To Brona, it looked like blood. She wanted to run. She wanted to scream.

Instead, something told her to open the basket, so she did. It's hard to override that kind of impulse.

Her eyes lit upon a pile of black silk thread and thicker, coarse twine covering the top of the basket. There were reams of it, curling as though the thread had been unravelled from something else, pressed down to fit inside. Nestled to the side, an empty conical spool. Beside it, a pincushion studded with six different size needles, a silver glint catching in the yellow artificial light. The thumping was now louder, steadier, more insistent, less muffled. There was something coming from beneath it. Brona, almost against her will, lifted the thread and the twine out. At the bottom of the basket, on fabric stained pink, a heart.

A heart she thought was human.

Brona slammed the basket shut and climbed back under her blanket. She covered her head like she was four and monsters had infiltrated her nightmares, breath hot against the fabric, her breathing slow and shaky. This wasn't right. This didn't make any sense. The ticking, beating, screaming of it, of the *heart* – though it couldn't be – forced her to look at it again.

Her eyes saw past the horror of it being a maybe-human heart and noticed it was clean. No blood anywhere on its bright red exterior. Just old silvery scars criss-crossing lightly on the surface of the heart and an open wound along the aorta, like sliced putty. Up close, it did not look like she imagined a heart would. It was sticky, for one.

Brona dropped it back into the basket and tried to sleep, jolted repeatedly out of crossing that precipice by a steadier thump that started just as sleep reached for her, until she gave up. Stood up. Emptied the basket onto the floor. Snatched the spool and tied the end of the thread around it and began to wind. She wound through her alarm and turned it off, turning off anything that might distract her until she had in front of her what could only be described as a bale of thread. Thick and shiny and perfectly uniform, dwarfing the spool with its sheer volume, so much more than what was in the basket in the first place. What looked like a lifetime of thread. More than she could ever think to use.

The heart had calmed itself by then, still beating and ticking gently. Brona had found a steady rhythm in its sound to aid her in winding. It seemed pleased – *could a heart experience literal emotions?* – that she was taking action. She laid the spool on its side and went to push it back under the bed. Taking the basket out would likely anger the heart – *could a heart be angry?* But no sooner had she pushed the basket into place and allowed the valanced sheet to fall, it beat louder and more insistently than ever before.

Brona wrenched the lid off again and stared down at it. It seemed so small and insignificant on the bottom of the basket, nestled next to the pincushion. Impossible that something so comparatively small to a body could be so responsible for life. The stain had begun to dry, settling into the cracks between the floorboards. Brona tried to find what it was, afraid someone's blood would be part of her home forever, seeping into the very foundations. But a search or two online turned up the concoctions used in embalming, and she became convinced it was formaldehyde. It meant someone, or something, had prepared it for her.

Even with this new knowledge, every time she closed the basket the heart would shout in anguish until she took the lid off again, staring at it helplessly. She searched the lining and the bottom of the basket, checked under the bed for any further information, but there was nothing else. Eventually, she took the spool and threaded the third biggest needle. She lifted the heart in her hand – it was warm as well as slightly sticky, though Brona tried not to think about that – and stitched the obvious wound closed. It was long and took her seven clumsy sutures, but in the end she tied off the thread and found a pair of scissors to cut it neatly. The heart quietened.

Satisfied that her problem was now solved, Brona put the heart back into the basket.

THUMP THUMP THUMP THUMP

She wrenched it open again and held it in her hands. She had done what it asked – *could a heart ask?* – and it seemed as though the heart should be happy now and Brona could go back to doing what she had been doing before, saturating in sadness in her bed. Her eyes alighted on the twine wound in a loop next to the spool, and Brona's hands moved almost independently of her to take the wicker basket lining and wrap the heart, securing it with twine. She was a dream-thing carrying out a dream-activity, and in this state she wrenched open the window latch and placed the heart-parcel on the windowsill. The heart became utterly silent.

Brona sat and waited.

She waited until the cut of sunrise when it came. A bird just like her bird, wings alight in copper flames, came to collect the package and carry it on.

Perhaps that could've been the end of it. But the next heart appeared in the same manner as the first, and this one had a name on it.

There was no thread this time – Brona had more than enough of that – and no twine, just a name tag tied around the vena cava. *Johnny Carey*, it said. In what would surprise no one – knowing what we know about the size of Ireland – Brona recognised the name as that of the grandfather of a school friend. He had been ailing with heart disease for some time, and this heart was not as perfect as the last. There were more cuts this time, frayed tears that did not seem related to the nature of his death, but that Brona stitched up anyway and sent it on its way.

She couldn't bring herself to bring herself to Johnny Carey's funeral when it was notified in the papers.

Again, that could've been the end of it. But the hearts came every night thereafter, sometimes two or three, all with names, some with initials, the hearts cut and torn and scarred in different ways. Brona's stitches become neater and she becomes more adept, learning the best way to tie off the thread, the neatest way to close up frays, how best to suture over scar tissue. She watched videos about it. She studied the anatomy of hearts. Still Brona did not know where the hearts went or what happened, but she knew in her own beating heart that their original owners were being laid to rest with every stitch. She was healing the lost, the lonely, the sad.

She just didn't know why.

The opposite of death – it's assumed – is life, and it goes on. Brona's nights were filled with stitching, and folk around her forgot about her. *She's never been the same since the bird died*, they said. *You'd think she'd be used to a few deaths by now.* Brona got used to the constant proximity of death in a small apartment of her own – the baskets, of course, followed – lonely and often cold, wrapped in a blanket and her hands in fingerless gloves, working through the nights and sleeping through the days, stitching hearts with shaking fingers and exhausted hands, not knowing why. Sometimes not knowing who. The nights spread into some daylight hours where she'd tried to find out who the hearts belonged to. Kept a list of whose hearts she thought she was healing, to some unknowable end.

The hearts kept coming. One came some years into her work that Brona held carefully in her hands, a tear falling as she thought of the time that had passed and the moments that she had lost. She sewed it up, one long, deep slice across the belly of the ventricles, but didn't put it on the sill. Instead, she walked across town and knocked on the door of the heart-owner. Brona hadn't seen him in some years, his face weathered by time, the features he'd given her an older mirror of her own. He looked surprised to see her, but invited her in for tea. Once she'd moved out of his home to find her own cold, lonely one, he had – it seemed – forgotten about her. A text here and there, but that was it. Brona held the mug the way she'd held his heart as she'd sewn it, felt the final pains and his final wishes, felt the things that all hearts couldn't let go of.

He asked – eventually, as was his way – why she was there. Brona could not make herself say it, but she thought it. *You'll be gone by morning.*

And he was.

She let the hearts pile up for a while after that one. Enduring the *I'm sorry for your loss*es and the silent, disapproving stares that demanded to know why she'd missed the last years of her father's life as Brona returned to society – for one night only – slipping out before she felt the need to scream at the pub full of well-wishing mourners that they needed to ask different questions, they needed to know what happened. But she didn't. She still didn't know herself.

Two years passed, maybe. A heart so small she could barely stand to look at it emerged from a basket one night. A tiny, fingernail-width cut blemished the underside of the pulmonary artery, so small Brona had to search for it, turning this heart over and over in her hands. It was Imbolc, the beginning of spring. The beginning of life. This one had ended. Brona lifted the basket and hurled it at the wall, splintering the wicker, and climbed into bed again, pulling the covers over her head. Monsters didn't come, but a voice spoke to her in a dream when sleep held her tightly. The heart was too tiny to interfere.

You carry their losses in your sorrow, the voice told her. *You carry them out of here.* She saw someone in that dream, a hazy figure. Though it did little to explain, it empowered her to continue for another year, and then the hearts stopped coming. For a month she could not sleep at night, waiting. When another month passed, heartless, Brona picked up the pieces of herself and returned to life. She felt how tired, how sick, how wanting she had been all those years when she filtered every regret and every sadness the hearts communicated to her through their injuries into her own heart. She found a job. She found a wife. For a year and a day no hearts came and Brona felt herself believing they never had. She stopped wondering what happened to those hearts and poured over the obituaries with her wife on a Sunday. She went to funerals. She refused to wonder.

They came back, the hearts. New ones, a year and a day from when they stopped, one night a month. Brona could live with once a month, hiding what she was doing from her wife with a pained smile, knowing she was not meant to tell anyone, praying to anyone that her wife would not see the copper-flamed bird pick up the hearts from the bay windowsill of their home. She could manage this. The small trickle of sadness. She had learned, with time, that she was healing with every stitch, passing the hearts on to the next cog in the machine who would take the dead where they were meant to go. The copper-flamed bird brought them onward every sunrise.

As it began, so it ended – with a beat.

On the final night, Brona heard a *thump*ing not in her room, but down the hallway. She slipped out of bed, her wife peacefully asleep still, her eyes closed and duvet tucked under her face. Brona looked at her for a moment, and padded down the hall towards the noise.

Stuffed inside the drum of the washing machine, a wicker basket. This one was different. She knew that the second she held it in her hands. This heart had one name on it, not that she needed a surname to confirm its owner. It was bright red and ravaged by sadness, she could see. Open wounds. Anger, resentment, loneliness. Scars criss-crossed and in varying states of healing, old silver scars torn open again, bursting at the seams. Many healed over time, the whisper of them tactile on the muscled surface. Brona knows the truth of each one. How each cut and tear and rip was a moment of sadness and brokenness for every heart she's healed. How some wounds matched those of the hearts that came before, including a tiny, fingernail-width scar behind the pulmonary artery.

With practised hands Brona stitched the final heart slowly – for she knew few things, but could know with certainty that it was the last one – and brought it to her room. She opened the window, laid it on the windowsill. Tucked herself into bed beside her wife, wrapped her arms around her and listened to her still-beating heart in her chest for the remaining hours of the night. Her bird would come by morning break. And she would be remembered.

PENELOPE

Chris Fitzpatrick

and then he said to me do you know how pretty you are and before I had a chance to say be off with you he plucked a sprig of purple heather and fixed it under the yellow ribbon just above my ear and I was red in the face

and I said he should know better not to be like this with me being a married woman

and then he smiled at me because he knew I did not mean what I said and then he lay back on the bank and put his hands behind his head and looked up at the sky and said this must be what heaven is like

and then I said I could not stay long as the boats would be returning and I would be needed for the gutting and the salting and he said just to lie with him until the boy on the cliff rang the bell to say the boats were here and it would be time enough to go then and then I lay beside him and I knew no one would find us here because we were in the old bog

and then he pointed upwards with his finger and said the words I had taught him for sun cloud blue sky heaven

and then he asked me what the word for grasshopper was because there were grasshoppers all around us and he laughed when I told him

and then he turned to me and asked me what the word for heart was and I did not answer because he could sing *súil súil eile*

and then my heart started to thump loudly and he half-sat up and leaned on one elbow and looked not at my face but at where my heart was and I did not turn red this time

and then he reached over and he opened the buttons of my cardigan and I pulled the rest of it open and I placed his hand over where my heart was and he whispered *croí* and he smiled and I smiled

and then he opened my blouse and he put his hand inside and I could feel his hand trembling and so I pulled him down on top of me and kissed him on the mouth and when I felt how he was hard I lifted up my skirt and helped him again and it was like when I jumped into the giant wave and could not breathe and it was strange to see his face so clear in the bright and not the shape of my husband in the dark and for there not to be a heavy quilt over us and a hard mattress under us but the sky and the heather

and when I smelled there was no smell of fish or porter only the smell of him

and then he asked me what I thought of him when I first saw him on the island and I said he looked like all the Yanks I had seen in photographs with his hat and suit and fancy brogues

and then I asked him what he thought when he first saw me and he said that when he saw me with the yellow ribbon in my hair he said to himself she is such a pretty one and when he found out I was the one to teach him Irish he was glad to pay what my husband asked for and to take the back room as well

and then I said do you have a sweetheart and he said yes but not as sweet as you and then I told him I had a daughter who was sixteen

and he said nothing but kissed me on the nose and I said she is with my mother over there and I pointed to the mainland and I said that is where I come from and then he kissed me on one ear and then on the other

and then he asked me if I loved my husband and I said he is a good man and I want for nothing

and then I asked him why he came here and he said when he
was in university he had come across the old stories that had
been translated and that when he read them he wanted to come
to where the stories were still being told

but even though you have been here all summer long you only
have a few words I said to him

and he said he would have learnt more words if I had been less
pretty and I said go away out of that and then he laughed and
I laughed

and he said again do you love your husband and I said do you
love your sweetheart and he said he liked her greatly and I said
it was the same between my husband and me

and then he said I should go to America with him and I said
I could never leave and then there was silence except for the
grasshoppers and skylarks

and then he said he wished he could stay but he could not and I
said even though this is heaven and I stretched my arms out wide

and he said even though this is heaven and then he bowed his
head and my blouse was wide open and he kissed me on my
breasts and I kissed the top of his head

and then he asked me if I believed in God

and to answer him I held his face in my hands and kissed him on the mouth and then I took the small purse out of the pocket of my skirt and opened it and showed him the pearl beads and he took them and put them around my neck

and then he asked me again to come with him to America but this time I put my finger over his lips to stop him and he kissed my finger and put it in his mouth

and then the ringing of the bell came from the cliff and I sat up and buttoned myself up and brushed down my skirt and cardigan and put on my shoes and ran down to the beach

and I could tell they had a great catch because the boats were low in the water and my husband was standing up in his boat waving his cap

and after the barrels were full of salted fish the big board was pulled out onto the road and my husband took out his melodeon and then the dancing began

and he was there but never once did he look me in the eye when we were dancing but he squeezed my fingers every chance he had

and before the dancing was over my husband asked me if I had a fever and I said no but he said it would be best for me to leave the dancing early because I had a high colour and when I went to bed I dreamed I was sailing on a ship to America with him

and the next morning my husband asked me if I would bring a jug of milk to the wife of his cousin before I set the table and I said yes and when I came back to the house I saw the door of the back room was open and his valise was gone

and then I ran down to the sea and I could see that he was in the boat sitting between my husband and his brother and his back was to the island

and when he turned around he was too far gone for me to make out his face but when my husband returned and was lying on top of me that night I could see it clearly again

CONNECTIONS CARVED IN STARLIGHT

Lark Morgan Lu

Dovetail was an out of the way recreation station that drifted between the residential neighbourhoods surrounding City-0042, itself a spiderweb metropolis conveniently placed between two resource-rich solar systems. It came up on Wren's recommendation search for clubs servicing non-cishet clientele. A week had passed since his Min-jun asked that they continue their relationship as friends and he couldn't bear to go back to the bar where he'd picked up Min-jun.

Dovetail pathed conveniently on Wren's way home. It'd be a short pod-hop from there to his residential node in case he over-indulged or, better yet, if he was to bring someone back with him. He worried at his lip and ran his hand through his black brush of hair before punching in the coordinates on his travel pod's touchpad.

Wren looked online for reviews on *Dovetail* as he waited to arrive. Almost nothing, relative to other stations of its clientele density – save one interesting comment, left anonymously.

Came here a few times for the impeccable service, but I think it's a front for something – a handful of the regulars are missing their left eyes?

Eye enhancements weren't particularly unusual, although replacing just one was strange.

The pod inserted itself into one of the few docking stations at *Dovetail* and, with the sound of rubbered suction, sealed itself against an entrance tunnel to let Wren inside. His pod door slid open. The air from the recreation station smelled only faintly of recycled breath; either the filters were top notch or the place was a ghost town.

No bouncer, human or artificial, came to greet him as he stepped into the entrance hallway. The biometric analysis system must've already scanned him upon entry. Wren worried he'd be underdressed at a place with such top-of-the-line technology – his day job as a logistics manager meant for a casual uniform of faded blue shirt and synthetic denim jeans. But clothes didn't make the man, so he pushed forward.

He passed by a woman on her way to reuse the pod he'd just left. She looked like her evening was ending, her eyes brimming with the delighted exhaustion of someone who had freshly restored her spirit and now was going to restore her body. Her head of turquoise curls bounced like a seafoam wave. She turned to glance his way as they crossed.

The woman had heather installments in both eye sockets, the aperture of her pupil narrowing and widening as it scanned over Wren's body. Were her implants related to this place? He didn't hide his public profile – Wren Zhang, 32, Bi, He/His, A+ blood,

Single and looking. He'd have to activate his own embeds to look her over the same way, if she even kept it publicly scannable.

'I haven't seen your face before.' Her voice had been smoothed out into an inauthentic syrup, though it made her no less soothing.

'Yeah, it's my first time here. Came up on Guidebook when I was looking for a new haunt.'

'I think you've found it. Why don't you ask the bartender for my schedule? We should get to know each other on my day off.'

'Do you work here?'

She laughed, although Wren had made no joke. 'I'll see you around, Wren.' Her heels clicked on the flooring like a hung phone call in a vintage movie.

Wren activated his own scanners on his palms and neck by the time he entered *Dovetail* proper through an onyx-black doorway that slid open as he approached. From the entrance, he could see a lounge-like first floor with a hint of more through an elevator on the far side of the room. He took a few photos with the embeds on his neck.

The entertainment venue looked hardly a quarter full, yet felt as warm as a packed dance floor. People lounged on white matte seats, some looking like they had just arrived, others looking ready to head home. To the side of the stage was the faux-wood bar, lined with stools and tubing to deliver drinks to the floors above.

A mix of nostalgic and current hits from icons played with no speakers in sight. Loud enough to make eavesdropping on conversations obvious, quiet enough to have them at all.

The bartender was laughing, fondly, at a joke of one of the patrons. He looked to be a man in maybe his mid-to-late twenties, wearing a vest and slacks with lines of neon caressing down his body. Wren sat at an empty seat and ran his palm scanner over the surface for a menu. His hand skidded over wax finish instead of plastic or glass. This was not fake wood.

A real wood bar was probably worth a small fortune. Yet the patrons here didn't seem all that wealthy, lacking skin replacements and embedded holographic projections. The person nursing their drink beside him (Socks, 22, Questioning, They/Them, [No blood type registered], Single not looking) had a smear of gel-slick hair covering their left eye, pressed flat enough that the slight concavity of an empty socket was unmistakable.

'Hi, uh, Socks–'

'Can you read my profile? Not looking.'

'Don't flatter yourself–'

The bartender glided to their side of the table. He smelled faintly of something that struck Wren's amygdala but skittered past his hippocampus, leaving him with a sense of nostalgia but no memory to accompany it. The bartender had no profile to speak of. No implants visible. A small nametag read "Kasey, he/him". 'Evening, Wren.' He slid over an old fashioned, Wren's drink of choice. 'Don't mind him, Socks. He's not looking for anything.'

Socks sulked into their electric blue drink. 'Maybe not now. He wouldn't sit beside me if he wasn't looking for something, though.'

'It might be because it's the only empty seat at the bar to-night.' Kasey reached over and soothed a thumb over Socks' hand. Socks didn't pull away, but gave a begrudging sort of shrug. They finished their drink in one swift swallow and then stepped off towards the exit with no motion of payment.

'I didn't order this drink,' Wren protested, even though he moved to sip. The whiskey was sweet and smooth – his pre-ferred style.

'Did I make it to your liking?'

'Yes, but–'

'Good.' Kasey grinned, his teeth bone-white and straight as razorblades. 'Please enjoy yourself as much as you'd like, ex-plore. There's a communal library on floor two and dancing in the penthouse. If you need anything, just wish it.' He floated away to another customer.

Wren nursed his old fashioned in the communal library for the evening. He made small talk with whomever seemed friend-ly enough, left his contact number with some of them. Here and there, he saw a few people with full or half eye replacements, and a fewer still of others like Socks, who either couldn't afford a replacement or used their socket as a fashion statement.

He started to leave several hours later, taking two books home with him: one on the evolution of symbiosis, the other on astrology. It was reaching closing time by the emptiness of the lounge. Kasey was still there, in a heated discussion with one of the patrons – (Julia, 47, Aroace, Fae/Faer, [No blood type registered], [No relationship status registered]).

'Must you bring it up constantly? All I'm saying on it is that we've colonised what, how many planets now? We're even starting intergalactic colonisation. Not a hint of intelligent life is there to be found. We're truly alone out here.' Fae banged faer fist on the wood hard enough to jangle faer layers and layers of jewellery, jade against turquoise.

'That depends on what we mean by intelligent, and what we mean by life. We've always only looked at what we could see.' Kasey responded, his mouth set in a politely irritated line.

'Oh not this again, Kasey. You'd think if there was life so radically different that it doesn't even do carbon and we haven't discovered it yet–'

'That's not what I'm saying. It's always the physical with us humans.'

'And you propose what? That something made out of radio waves is going to saunter into your little club? We have all sorts of queers here but I'll eat my stiletto–'

'Julia, Julia–' Kasey was laughing now, a sound of hapless, friendly bafflement. His eyes caught Wren as the latter had moved towards the exit. 'Oh, are you heading out, Wren? Have a good evening. Hope to see you back soon.'

Wren glanced back at Kasey, then Julia, then Kasey again. '…What about my tab?'

Julia was the one to laugh then. 'I guess no one told him? There ain't a tab here. You'll get a ring when you're home.'

Wren went home empty-handed but with a pleasant buzz. It'd been a long time since he'd been anywhere that welcomed him with such little suspicion, and it mollified the sting of a lonely bed. He'd have to go again and maybe next time he'd be luckier.

Sometime the next day, Wren could find no sign of that anonymous comment anywhere, not even in the archives of Guidebook's website.

It took a few trips for Wren to understand *Dovetail*, just as the anonymous review noted. One, there was only one bartender, Kasey, who served only one drink – the favourite of whomever he served.

Two, there was no tab, only subsequent bills after you left – the biometric scanners were the real deal if they could find his e-bill address, and Wren suspected Kasey might actually own the recreation station outright with independent wealth.

Three, approximately a quarter of all the regulars he saw sported an installment or complete removal of their left eyes – although most of those had full installments.

Four, the regulars without left eyes kept to each other, came at odd hours, and had long conversations with Kasey in tones too quiet for eavesdropping.

(Five, Socks had nothing out for Wren personally. They trusted no one save Kasey and a few one-eyed regulars.)

By Wren's third visit, he felt he had a good idea of the layout. The woman he first met, Valor, joined him in the library that evening. She was an attorney for one of the larger companies at City-0042, specialising in interplanetary logistics law. She melted over one of the reading benches, right over Wren's lap, and sipped at her wine.

'Valor, do you mind if I ask you something?'

'Oh, going to let me be your wingwoman again tonight?' Her glossy lip quirked.

'…I actually wanted to ask about eyes.'

Valor sighed. 'Is that damn review still up? I figured Kasey would've buried it by now.'

'Wait, buried? I just figured it was a nasty comment on a coincidence and then it was deleted.'

She shook her head, her spirals of hair spilling over her shoulders as she moved to sit back up. 'Have you considered visiting the bar more often? I think you'll get more information there.'

Wren paused before he next spoke. She knew something but insisted he figure it out himself. Valor tapped her left eye in wait, manicured nail clicking against glass. He let out a sigh. 'Fine... It might be easier for me to find someone there anyways.'

'You know who to call if you need some help with introductions.'

He smiled a little then. 'Not after the last time! She went home with you instead!'

'It's not my fault I'm so pretty!'

If Kasey noticed Wren staking out his bar like a statue parked in front of a temple, he didn't comment on it. Nothing was off limits in terms of topic matters with Kasey, or with the other regulars at the bar. They spoke on local politics, like the recent referendum to grant sufficiently advanced algorithms voting rights, and personal lives, like making sure Socks had enough money to afford their medication. Wren learned Socks' drink wasn't alcoholic at all, and Julia could outdrink anyone at the table put together with the speed fae put away bourbon.

He had no luck convincing anyone for anything more than a pity date. It wasn't so bad when he was there, among friendly faces, but it stung worse and worse on the trips home.

In the second week of regular bar stakeouts, Wren noticed Kasey slip a piece of paper to one of the regulars who had both their eyes (Asmee Brown, -82, Het, She/Her, A security Bug If I Ever Saw One–, Seriously looking).

The next time he saw her, a week later, she looked the same as she always had – save for the slight swelling around her left eye. When Wren commented on it, Asmee smiled and said she'd just replaced it as the old one had started to develop cataracts, and the tissue was still healing from the implanting surgery. Funny, Wren considered, because Asmee had never mentioned that eye giving her trouble before.

'Did you know before we started living outside of planets, we used to have surgeries that left scars? Of course, that sort of butchery is illegal now, last one I heard of was my great-grand-mother. Medicine has gone a really long way,' she chittered over her sangria.

Wren fought to catch Kasey's gaze, like an accusation.

Kasey never looked his way.

It was a month after his first visit when Wren stayed late at the bar for the first time. Really late. His latest attempt to find love with Asmee had failed (although he hadn't really expected it to succeed) and he felt quite sore about his dry spell. As always, Kasey stayed with him, chatted about everything.

Wren wasn't sure when it happened but at some point it was just himself and Kasey in the otherwise empty *Dovetail*. The lights overhead had shut down in preparation for closing, but Wren didn't quite feel ready to head to his too-empty bed.

'Have you ever considered extraterrestrial life, Wren?' Kasey asked in the dim.

'I suppose, once or twice. Julia was right, I think, the first time I was here. The human civilisation is an amoeba, swallowing up solar systems, but we haven't found anything resembling our spread.' Wren ran his fingers over the worn wood. 'But you're not wrong, either. If there is life out there, it'd have to look like something… I guess maybe it doesn't even look like anything. Certainly not anything we'd recognise as life.'

Kasey ran a cloth over a few glasses even though he had appliances to do that for him. He did this absentmindedly, with a professional movement that spoke of many years at his labour. 'If we're the only things out there, living, loving, with all our flaws… We certainly don't conduct our civilisation like the shining example of it. But let me ask you something else, Wren. How would you justify that, if we weren't alone? If you could speak at all to whatever might be out there, how would you justify us?'

'Is this what you speak of with all the others, Kasey?'

Kasey was silent for a long time, his smile faltering slightly. His gaze turned to the exit with a look of deep longing, and then he looked back at Wren with those warm, dark eyes of his. 'I have to close, Wren. This was a lovely talk. Perhaps we could continue tomorrow night. I'll be here.'

Wren wanted to refuse, in that moment. Threaten to write a report to Guidebook and every other station review site. Maybe even program a script that would repost the eyes thing every time Kasey paid off whomever he paid off. But then the little community that had so embraced him, what would come of it? The thought drifted into his mind like *Dovetail* into neighbourhoods. If anyone had regretted what happened, no one had shown it, not even the ever-spurious Socks.

If anything, it seemed the loss made them all bind tighter together.

Wren didn't realise when his head hit the pillow of his bed, or even that he had left *Dovetail* at all, but he did at some point. In his dreams, he was as large as City-0042, his many limbs snaking through each and every person who had ever seen him. In time, he would swallow his meal whole. He woke with a terrible headache, his sensors sparking against his skin like they had been overcharged.

He checked himself in the bathroom mirror and pondered at the red swelling against the implants through the fog of hangover. It wasn't unusual for implants to cause the occasional irritation where machine interfaced with biology. He pondered, too, at the fuzziness of the night before, recalling only the warm comfort of a bartender on an otherwise lonely night. Wren probably needed to cut back on drinking. He wasn't a young twenty-something anymore.

Wren came to *Dovetail* whenever he felt lucky, or if he just wanted some company in his new friend group. City-0042 was akin to a little galaxy in and of itself, with the starlight of various businesses exploding onto the scene or winking out of existence maintaining a constant pulse of energy in the inhabitants. Yet he found no other places quite with *Dovetail*'s friendliness.

Guidebook didn't recommend *Dovetail* very often to people, or, at least, that's what Wren concluded after another week or so since his embarrassingly drunk night. Most people looking for entertainment would take a pod into the main network of City-0042, not the residential sparsity surrounding it.

Then, a piece of paper slid over under the coaster of his first old fashioned for the night. A scannable code, like an inkblot. He pressed his right palm sensor against it and sipped with the other. A contact profile came downloaded into his mind, slid in like an epiphany. One moment he knew Kasey only by his nametag, next he had a picture-perfect memory of his call number and residential node address, and with this information Kasey's voice – *Would you allow me to fall in love with you? Come to my door. We can be a home for a time.*

The whole club felt deafening, claustrophobic, each figure passing, even people whose faces didn't know him beyond his public profile, was undoubtedly and without warning judging him. Watching him. Questioning him on what he'd choose.

Socks brushed past him on their way to a chair, and he flinched. They flinched in response and shuffled to a more distant chair before glancing at the paper under the coaster. That look was unmistakably suspicious. Kasey glided towards Socks, put a hand on their shoulder, reassuring. They relented only a little. Wren left, still stone-cold sober, and Kasey didn't call for him.

He called a pod and stepped in, slumped into the lounge chair and hovered his fingers over the pad to navigate his way home. But he hesitated. Did he really want to go to back to his empty bed, again, when there was someone who finally had some interest in him? Someone who offered him the sort of connection he had been looking for, seemingly everywhere, with chance by chance slipping through his fingers? He looked at his reflection against the glass of the navigation pad, at his dark eyes gleaming against the bright screen, star-like, and made his decision. Wren called up the contact number and was put through immediately, even though he knew Kasey was working.

Kasey's voice was smooth and far away. There was no ambient sound of music, clinking glass, laughter or conversation on his end. Maybe Kasey's devices were top of the line – same as anything else in *Dovetail*. 'Hi, Wren.'

'Shouldn't you be working?'

'I never work. I hope you don't mind Socks. They're protective.'

'So I gather. What do you want from me?'

'I only want to be in love with you.'

'…Okay. I'll see you at your place.'

Kasey's residential node was quite far from *Dovetail* – in fact, it was one of the most distant nodes surrounding City-0042. It was a self-contained cluster in and of itself. A gaudy amount of wealth must've been used monthly to keep the cluster stable and to avoid air leaks. Wren could even see *windows*.

His pod pressed into the docking platform. Kasey stood there to greet him, extended a hand and helped him into the hallway that led deeper into the house.

Kasey held onto his hand all the way to their bed.

Wren never knew a man who loved him as earnestly as Kasey. They explored every inch of each other – Kasey appeared to have no installments anywhere. His skin was warm and unmarred save for two crescent moons of scar tissue on Kasey's chest.

Wren didn't notice when his left eye was taken precisely. They were holding each other like interlocked chains. The bed was pleasant and warm and the sheets smelled like them. Kasey whispered the request into Wren's ear and chased each word with a kiss. Wren sighed, held Kasey close, and asked if he could at least know what he did with them. Kasey pressed his yes into the juncture where Wren's neck met his shoulder. Wren at last assented and closed his eyes. Somewhere between them, a noise like a glass door sliding closed.

Wren opened his remaining eye. Kasey's face – the entire room – had shifted slightly rightwards. Kasey's left hand held a small, pale orb, with tiny flecks of grey and a spiderweb of red. There was no pain.

'Thank you,' Kasey whispered. They shared a kiss, Kasey's hands stroking into his shoulders, affectionate and loving and kind. Then Kasey left. Wren enjoyed the view until his silhouette disappeared out the door and down a hallway. Wren stood and followed.

They wandered into a room with a wall of glass. This would've cost a fortune to install; the sealant alone would need regular application and cost his quarterly wages. This distant from the main hub of the city, the galaxy seemed ready to swallow them.

Wren watched Kasey pull out a jar of clear gel, glue-like, and spill it over his eye. Preservative. Kasey then reached up and strung the eye up on a garland – and that's when Wren noticed them. Dozens, perhaps hundreds of them, eyes floating in their sacs of preservative gel like amphibious eggs. A soft light emanated from lighting above, just enough to make them shine.

'What is this?' Wren asked, hardly above a whisper.

Kasey had no gaze for Wren, for his eyes were captured by the brightness in the void beyond the window. '…What do you do, Wren, when there *is* life out there?' Kasey murmured.

'What–'

'When it's been speaking to us all this time, asking if someone, anyone could hear? How do you say, "I'm here" to something that speaks only with the slowly spilling glitter of a galaxy?'

Kasey was building a constellation with their eyes. Wren watched Kasey study the stars and felt disbelief, understanding and, finally, a tenderness that he had missed dearly. While the stars had twinkled upon humanity for eternity, someone – at least this one man – had figured out how to glimmer back. Kasey moved to his own collection of glistening lights in the dark and moved them in patterns, Ursa Majors and Gemini of his own, smiling out into space with all the fondness of a long-standing love.

FELLOW IN THE FIRMAMENT

Cormack Baldwin

The stars were changing again, and Richard Miles was sick of it. It was brazen at this point. The furtive changes meant to stoke paranoia, to force him to question whether he had a true grip on reality, had been cast aside for the sake of dramatics. He could watch points wink into being and swirl into semi-permanent locations as if being drawn by a magnet. He just didn't know what it meant.

It had been another thing at the beginning, two weeks ago. The first hint had been the ribbon of aurora impossibly projected against London clouds. He'd attributed it to hallucination. The next night, he'd wondered if there was some airplane show going on. The third night, he searched newspapers for references to a festival of lights. He denied it until he couldn't anymore. He had exhausted every implausible possibility, and accepted that it was part of the impossible that haunted his life. The aurora had been the signal at the start of a code, like someone pushing up their glasses before beginning a cant. A command. *Listen.*

To what? he silently demanded of the shifting stars. Of course he was listening. He didn't have a *choice* but to listen. He had been listening since he'd met his imaginary friend as a child. It, or whatever tendril of itself that had broken off inside of him, made certain that it would not be ignored. But he had gone from child to teenager to world-weary college dropout, and it had gone from harmless tricks to rewriting the astronomical history of mankind. Assuming, that was, that it existed outside of the bends in reality around him. Assuming it existed at all.

Listen, came the whisper in the depths of his mind. The last star glided into place, and the lightshow began. The new stars twinkled in and out of existence like a faulty "open" sign. It should have given them form, and form should have given them meaning. From this billion-mile view, each one should have writ as clear as a billboard across the sky. But the shapes were tangled, random. It was a connect-the-dots puzzle without numbers.

Hissing a sigh between his teeth, he began taking the photos. Most of them, developed in his closet-cum-darkroom later that night, would probably end up being nonsense. Even with the right lens and the right timing, trying to capture pinpricks against a twilight blanket was a fool's errand. Light bounced and scattered off the city smog, leaving a haze that rendered all but the brightest stars invisible. That was if the stars would even stay put to be captured on some mortal's concoction of cellulose and chemicals. His old friend's opinion on photographs was just as enigmatic as anything else about it. Its tricks might stay in all of them, or none at all, or a single frame in a batch of twenty. Just enough to leave him wondering whether or not to trust what he saw.

Because you're a lunatic, he reminded himself as he stowed his photography equipment and made his way back to his flat. Because he was the consequence, the nameless victim of pulp magazines, driven to madness by a childhood encounter with something beyond this reality. No, he wouldn't have been afforded that dignity. The pitying curtain call was for young white academics. He would have been cast as the dangerous islander, worshipping that which was meant to be feared. Ignore that he had been eight years old, and only drawn to the company of imaginary friend. Ignore the fact that it had found him in the suburbs of London. Ignore that the world did not work that way, that those who thought it did were mired in a paranoia even deeper than his.

But his old friend did not put much stock in the narratives of frightened men. The photographs developed all the same. And Richard Miles, possible lunatic, watched as the stars twinkled through the haze of blood-red light.

And that is how he found himself trying to draw lines between points that may as well have been produced by birdshot punching through the night sky. Perhaps the truest sign of lifelong damage from a childhood encounter with the unknowable was his confidence that answering this one mystery might tie up others. Or his initial certainty that this could be answered at all. That, at least, had waned the longer he worked.

His progress thus far was a raging headache and a series of scribbles that resembled the thrashing of a beached sea creature. He had to wonder if his old friend was punishing him for failing to decode what it certainly considered obvious. He had to wonder if he was punishing himself.

He resisted the urge to tear the paper into a thousand pieces as he set it aside and grabbed a blank sheet to begin again. He traced a cross over each star he could see through the paper, set the photograph aside, and tried a new set of lines. A to B. B to C. He could do this all day if he had to. Not as if he had a job anymore, or school. He was working on the former, even as the latter smouldered behind him. All of his old friends (the human variety) were still on their tracks to becoming journalists, moving from A to B, B to C. One thing after another.

He thought of constellations. The invisible lines that tied stars so distant they only barely knew each other's light. A memory, blurry with youth, of a hand on his shoulder, another pointing out star by star. Pegasus, Cygnus, Ursa Major. Couldn't he see them? He'd squinted, trying to make a horse out of the handful of dots. They'd stayed as they were, unblinking. He'd read every book he could find on the stars, but even memorising the blocky shape of Pegasus didn't make it appear in the sky.

What appeared in the sky was paranoia and lies. Pegasus had probably moved out of the way.

Richard held the half-filled paper up to the light and tried to force the dots and lines into a shape that made sense. Partial answers came together and fell apart in his mind's eye. If he tilted it, he could almost imagine the sun rising over a bay. A row of stars outlined undulating sand dunes. An arc over top made up the sun. Libra-like Vs could even be interpreted as seagulls calling over their starry domain. Stupid, perhaps, but at least it was something.

He put down the paper and filled in the remaining lines. It was sloppy, like a child's crayon drawing. It did, however, make sense, and that was more than the previous ones. A beach was a place, a physical location. One could go to a beach.

It was then a matter of *which* beach. Even if he were to assume that it referred only to the shores he could access, stuck in the city without enough money for bus fare most days, there was no shortage of lakes, ponds, and shoulders of the Thames, not to mention the actual ocean. The headache that had eased its grip as he'd drawn the scene roared back to life. He rubbed the bridge of his nose. Coffee. He would make himself a drink, and he would return to the stars.

When he returned with a steaming mug of something too strong to even call itself coffee, the only thing that remained of the papers was the sting of absinthe-scented smoke and a small pile of chemical-green sand.

This was war.

The stars were changing again, but this time Richard was prepared. It wasn't just the camera slung around his neck anymore, or the briefcase leftover from his student days, filled with pens and papers and all sorts of other things that could disappear in a wisp of smoke. It was the book pressed between his left elbow and his ribs – *Practical Astronomical Navigation*.

The book veered from dry to insulting to back again, but that still held the weight of nostalgia in his hands. Its "short" history section, which spanned nearly half the onion skin-thin pages, had focused largely on the Vikings, reluctantly touched on China, and only deigned to discuss the *pasifika* at the very end. It was an odd feeling, hearing even begrudging admiration filtered through the language of academia. Perhaps that was why he had kept it, even as his studies drifted further and further away. He could be alone in his classes, could be denied jobs, respect, autonomy, could be cut off from everything he had once been, but by God, at least he had the stars. And he was going to get them back.

He stood on the hill of the park, watching the stars swirl into and out of place as he opened the book to the first guides. The pictures appeared in the form of woodcut-like scratches and dots. A white fist stood against a pointillist black background. *The fist makes a ten degree angle. Stack fist over fist from the horizon to the North Star to find your latitude.* He scanned the sky for the telltale pointers, expecting none. Orion had been decimated in the change, and he'd watched Cygnus come apart in a burst of stellar feathers.

Yet there was Ursa Major, albeit halfway across the sky from where he would have anticipated. Its nose still pointed to a lone star. Richard set the book facedown on the briefcase and squinted at the horizon. By the time he had one fist resting on it, the error was obvious. According to the new star map, London hung at barely ten degrees of latitude, somewhere near Ghana. He held out the other fist, half expecting it to change dramatically between the two. Still ten degrees.

He didn't know what do to about it, but any guess was better than none. He was supposed to be at fifty degrees, so he would go toward fifty degrees. Hopefully his old friend was just as uncertain about distance, and this was not going to be the beginning of the long walk to the North Pole. He tucked the book back into place under his arm, hoisted the case, and began the trek north. The park's refuge of greenery soon bled into the network of concrete sidewalks that knew no cardinal direction, only the sprawl of urban expansion.

It was too late for a crowd, but there were enough people for Richard's heart to skip a beat as he tried to keep track of both them and the rising star. Men in shirtsleeves shouldered past him like he was a ghost, not even looking up at his yelp when one elbowed his camera and sent the book clattering to the ground.

The book was unharmed outside of a thin layer of city grime. Yet vertigo twisted Richard's stomach as he stood. The ground underneath him shifted as if on a turntable – no, not the ground. The sky. The stars burst from their temporary cells and raced to new positions with trails of aurora green.

Richard squeezed his eyes shut, but he could *feel* the movement, as if each star were tracing a path in his veins. Polaris fell. Ursa Major dissolved, shot by Orion's newly formed bow. Richard stuck out an arm in hopes of catching something, anything that would stop his world from spinning. Instead–

'Watch it!' someone snapped.

Richard's eyes flew open, which proved to be a mistake. The flashing had begun. 'I'm, I'm sorry,' he stammered to the woman who had narrowly avoided his outstretched arm.

She sniffed, then lifted her chin. 'What are you doing? Just been gaping at the sky, then feel the need to assault passersby? I ought to call the police.' She didn't wait for his dry-mouthed answer before storming off.

'You don't see it?' he whispered to her back.

Of course not. Why would she see it? Why would anyone other than Richard see it? Why would the universe afford him even that? He reached again for a handhold, but the buildings around him seemed unspeakably distant. He settled on tugging his jacket closer.

He needed to get out. Orion sparkled like a gem on the horizon. No, he wouldn't look. He couldn't look. He needed to get home, whether or not the thing puppeting the stars would be there. He turned and ran.

The stars followed.

Like a predatory beast, they pounced across the sky, until the new stars appeared in front of him as a singular point of painful brightness. He didn't know what would happen if he were to approach it, but his heart constricted with a surge of fear.

He turned again. He ran again.

The stars returned to their mock positions, twinkling when he reached the street corner he'd just been on. If it was a reward, he couldn't see for what. But there was no going farther south, and he didn't know what would be to the north. He turned, hoped that the blinking crosswalk was real along with the empty road, and took off in a new direction.

The stars began their sickening ballet above him. The world rocked like a ship to sea. He missed a step in an attempt to correct for the movement of what was once a static point, and narrowly avoided toppling to the ground face- and camera-first. No time for mistakes. No time for broken equipment and hitching breath. No time for glass in his hands.

He didn't know where he was going, and the realisation scared him more than the cascade of light around him. Those who did not have a goal would be herded toward someone, something else's.

That goal became clear soon enough, forcing him to skid to a rocky stop. Too late. His feet fell out from under him, and for the first time that night the vertigo was real. He grunted as the small of his back hit a stone, but his coat had gotten the brunt of the damage. If he could run, that was all he cared about. He forced himself to kneel.

Another wave of disorientation, and he fell onto his hands and knees. With shock but not fear, he craned his neck up at a constant sky.

Pegasus. Cygnus. Ursa Major, pointing toward a static North Star at just the right spot in a clear sky. A reward. A break in the delusion. It didn't matter. He traced invisible constellations with his eyes, finding comfort in the random curves and angles. The sky was alright, even if he wasn't.

It must have been a harmless prank. Even if he resented his old friend for that, it wasn't the worst it could do. He was not so far gone as to consider himself lucky, but at least he'd been dropped somewhere familiar. The scenery, lit in stark silver, itched with memory. He sat on the flat shore, arched over by the curve of a bridge. A few late seagulls still called tentatively over the waters. Serpentine Lake, he believed. That was fine. He could navigate from there.

He stood. His legs still shook with the adrenaline, his hair was puffed about him like a cloud fallen to Earth, and his eyes were no doubt wild with fear. No wonder that the woman had been surprised. He leaned forward, peering into his reflection in the water.

The water peered back.

The deceitful sky watched from the water, its false stars gazing up at their counterparts with empty irises. From the centre stared a single massive eye, unblinking and aurora green.

It was not a feeling of falling. It was a feeling of no longer being. Senses dissolved as reality twisted in on itself. That which was once Richard broke apart and cowered in disparate corners of the single, universal lie. There was no room for doubt. There was only doubt. The world was one of broken mirrors and sparking stars. Sickening familiarity, no longer shrouded but accentuated by youth, filled his throat like bile. He had seen this before.

This was not the face of madness, it was the face of a god.

With an absinthe ribbon, the stars began to move.

LAKE UNKNOWN

James Dwyer

Jek and Den gave the woman one last chance to change her mind. They'd explained that it was almost certain she'd be killed. Hardly anyone survived it. Either the swamp got them, or the forest got them, or they got eaten by cackling birds. It was Jek and Den's job to make sure none of that happened, but even the ones they guided safely to the lake usually ended up dead in some spectacular way.

'You're certain you want to go through with this?' Jek asked again. 'I mean, we'll give you back your coin. There's still time for you to see sense.'

Jek's brother, Den, twitched uncomfortably at the idea of returning money. It didn't matter that no one ever changed their mind at this stage, on the very threshold of their dreams, so no refunds had been needed. Still, Jek liked to make sure the clients were sure. A verbal cleansing of responsibility. It wasn't the easiest way to make a living – leading idiots to their deaths – but it had its benefits, and it made Jek and Den happy. Each stage of the journey was dangerous, but every time they walked it there was also some new beauty to be found.

The woman was staring at Jek as he thought about that. She even grinned at him as if she could see what he was picturing. There weren't many women who'd smile at Jek Brawler. He was ugly enough to sour a baby's milk inside the tit just by winking at it. This woman was a strange one though, all painted lines and coloured wraps. Jek smiled back at her with his fistful of missing teeth.

'Your concern is kind, Mister Brawler,' she said firmly. 'But this is the path I have chosen, so this is the path I shall walk.'

Her voice sent shivers through his fingertips. She was a strange one alright, but then again there weren't many normal folk who went strolling around looking for Lake Unknown – apart from him and Den. Jek tipped his head towards his brother.

'You hear that, Den? She called me Mister. Why don't you do that?'

'I thought your name was Jek,' Den muttered, confusion squeezing his face. Wasn't the brightest torch, was Den. Probably about the only person in the world that was uglier than Jek, too. Maybe that was why he loved him so much.

'Yeah, well, I'm thinking about changing it to Mister. What do you think?'

'Can I still be Den?'

'No, you'd have to be Jek.'

His brother's face collapsed with panic, the joke missing the poor man and wandering off to die inside the swamp.

'I'll tell you what,' Jek said to calm him, 'how about you be Den, I be Jek, and we go lead this nice woman to her death. Sound good?'

Den beamed his relief. All those were things that he knew how to do. 'Sounds good, Jek.'

The Swamp of Songs was sometimes called the Screaming Swamp. This wasn't the swamp's fault. The song it naturally made – or maybe not so naturally – was mostly due to the wind that constantly crashed its way through the trees. Some clients liked to terrify themselves by saying it was the rattling of lost bones. To Jek and Den it was music, a pleasant drumbeat for their march. Their march through the marsh.

'Hey, Den.'

'Yeah, Jek?'

'We're marching through a marsh.' Den broke down in pieces laughing at that and Jek's smile nearly cracked his face. 'Look at us, we're marshing!'

Both brothers needed to stop their hike and give that the proper laughter it deserved. The woman joined in with a crooked grin. Maybe she didn't get the joke. Jek was about to explain it, but she saved him the need.

'A swamp is not a marsh, Mister… Jek.' She smiled at Den as she said that, but both brothers stopped their chuckling to scowl at her. She looked so damn out of place in this "swamp" of musty green. She was wrapped in silks of sunlight, all bright oranges, yellows, and gold. And she had paintings on her arms as well, of haunted purples, blacks, and blue.

'We've been guiding idiots through this swamp, Madam… Pira,' Jek said back, 'for almost ten years now. I think we'd know what it is or isn't.'

Pira bowed her head to show she intended no disrespect. 'All I meant to say was that swamps usually begin as lakes, until forests grow in them and dry them out. Whereas marshes begin as flatland that becomes flooded, and they don't generally grow trees.'

Jek frowned around at the creaking trees, and the twists of bark did their best to glower back. To him, there was too much water here to call anything a forest. Too much hungry mud to eat you up. If him and Den didn't have that map they bought way back, then they'd be planted here like everything else. That was why this place was called the Screaming Swamp, by the way. From idiots too proud or poor to pay the Brawler brothers to guide them safe. Get lost out here and the swamp takes payment instead. It eats you up, slow and steady, enough to keep a man screaming for weeks.

'Let's keep moving,' Jek mumbled. 'Still got another few hours of marching before we camp.'

'A few hours of marshing,' Den sniggered. This got both brothers giggling again and they enjoyed the rest of the journey like they always did. Jek led the way with Pira following close, and Den watched the rear, making sure their client stayed on track.

They made it to the first day's campsite without a hitch. It had been a while since they'd lost anyone to the swamp, but there were always some idiots who figured they knew best. Pira didn't look like one of these, but she didn't look all that pleased by Jek telling her that they were stopping either.

'We still have several hours until sunset, Mister Jek,' she said. 'I would appreciate it if we continued on.'

Den ignored her and started busying himself with their packs. He'd have a fire going in no time and he'd supper up some tasty stew. Damn fine cook, was Den.

'Appreciate all you want, Madam Pira, but this is where we camp. You're free to continue on alone but we'll be at the Faded Forest soon, and that isn't anywhere you'd want to be at night. Besides, this is a good camp. It's dry, it's sheltered, we're in the perfect spot to hear the song, and we've a latrine dug back there behind those trees, so you have somewhere private to go piss and shit.'

At the mention of the latrine, Den stopped what he was doing and unbuckled his belts.

'There you go,' Jek added. 'Den can even show you how it's done.'

Pira just tilted her head at Jek as Den disappeared behind the trees. He was impressed that she didn't sneer at him or feign disgust. You'd be surprised by how many people liked to pretend they didn't shit.

'The perfect spot to hear the song?' she asked. She seemed to accept that they were staying here, so she curled herself down to a graceful sit. Every time she made a move, Jek felt even more big and clumsy. That was one advantage of being ugly; everything else looked more beautiful by compare. Not a bad way to live a life, Jek reckoned, to spend it admiring beauty.

'Yep,' he said, 'this is the Swamp of Songs, after all.' He waited and listened, just in case the swamp might respond, but they were early yet. 'We've been doing this for years, remember, and there's a reason we keep coming back.'

'All those years,' she whispered, 'and you've never been tempted to look into Lake Unknown?'

'We can talk about the lake if we make it there,' he told her. 'Not everyone does, and usually it's because they're too busy thinking about tomorrow instead of paying attention to today.'

'I apologise. Please, tell me about the song.'

'You'll hear it soon, and we're just far enough away that you won't be tempted to wander close. This swamp goes all the way around the lake. Things that big need a lot to eat.'

'You're saying that the swamp lures prey here to be eaten, by... singing when it's hungry?'

'The swamp is always hungry, and it's me and Den that call it singing. There's more melody to that idea than thinking of it as bog-farted gas.'

'Bog-farted gas!' Den cracked up every time Jek said that. Probably a good thing for the lady that Den had just finished doing what he'd been doing. Otherwise she might've gotten a song of Den's own devising, one blasted merrily from his arse.

'You are interesting men,' Pira told them. She didn't say it as an insult, but Jek shrugged the words away nonetheless. He'd been called plenty worse in his time, and he'd toughened himself to take it. Pira's words, however, sounded dangerously like praise. He wasn't sure he'd like for her to like him. It would make things more complicated when she died.

The song they heard that night was among the most magical Jek had known. Every time he heard it was special. Sitting safe and strong beside his brother, it was the best of times a man could have. Sometimes a client spoiled it, either by getting captured by the siren's snare, wandering off into the dark to die, or else by vocalising how it made them feel. But Jek didn't care. He only wanted to enjoy the experience with his brother. The rest of the world could rot. That night, however, Pira managed to elevate the song from beautiful to glorious.

Jek had seen a man make music from rubbing glasses filled with water once. Each had different volumes and each glass he rubbed gave off a unique pitch. That was the closest he could come to describing the kind of song the swamp made. Only it was accompanied by the beat of trees, and the swish of grass, and the occasional splash. It was a symphony of the highest form, and when Pira stood to listen, Jek worried that he'd have to tackle her to keep her safe. But she wasn't caught in the music's spell – or at least not in the way that people usually were.

Rather than race off into the swamp to heed the song's deadly call, Pira began to dance. In perfect harmony, all twisting wrists and twirling hips, she became the far more mesmerising danger. Jek had never seen a body move like that, the way her limbs would flick and her robes would whisk. He and Den were completely bewitched. She could have commanded them to do anything at that moment and they would've done it without a moment's pause. Only after it was over, once twilight faded and the song settled into sleep, could Jek think enough to understand that Pira's dance had in no way been for him or Den. Her dance was for the swamp. Her movements had been the song. Jek went to sleep that night wondering why this mysterious woman even needed them as guides.

The next morning, Jek was back to normal. Pira's dancing wasn't mentioned. It just became a treasure they would keep. Their morning meal was quick and their hiking pace increased once they cleared the Swamp of Songs. The Faded Forest was next. They had to make it to the second campsite before sunset once again, although for far more pressing reasons. Same as the first site, the camp outside the forest was chosen for its beauty, but it was also the only safe spot for them to stop between the Swamp of Songs and Lake Unknown.

On any good day, the distance between campsites wasn't a problem. It only became a problem if some fool client started lagging, or sprained their ankle, or touched anything they shouldn't touch. Pira didn't seem the kind to suffer any of these misadventures, but you could never know, so for Jek it was always good to do the going while the going was doing good.

The dangers were less obvious in the woods compared to the swamp. Mostly the risk was in getting lost. Few were the landmarks to distinguish one set of trees from the next. Only that map that Den had purchased all those years back outlined the secret trails. It still made them laugh when they thought back to how annoyed Jek had been. To find that his brother had spent a full month's wages on a worthless scrap of map. It was only to teach Den a lesson that Jek had made this journey that first time. He'd expected they'd get stuck in the swamp within three or four steps, so he'd brought plenty of rope and an even greater amount of smug for when the map turned out to be fake. The further and further they got, however, avoiding all the dangers infamous with the path to Lake Unknown, Jek came to realise the true value of what Den had bought. Ten years later they had made a fine fortune doing what they do. Some would say they'd earned enough not to work as guides on this route anymore, but then some might ask back, what else were they supposed to do instead?

They made it through most of the Faded Forest and on to the second campsite with time to spare. Pira had been told not to touch anything and not to slow her pace. She had taken that advice seriously, so now she was still alive. Still alive to see the second wonder Jek and Den had to show.

Their camp was in a small clearing this time, with no shelter to speak of, but they needed to keep just the right distance away from trees. If it rained, it rained. Today the sky was crisp and cloudless, so Jek reckoned they might stay dry. They lit another fire and Den cooked another stew – after once more showing Pira where the latrine was dug, this time behind some rocks – and Jek waited for the lights.

Pira watched him closely, her eyes lingering on him whenever she thought he wouldn't see. But Jek was good at noticing. It was what made him a great guide and it was what brought him the most joy. A lot of people didn't spot the best of beauty because they weren't properly looking. Jek looked. And he found it more often than not. Den sometimes had trouble seeing what Jek could see, but he helped his brother in every way he could. Sharing those beauties made him love each moment more.

'So, Mister Jek,' Pira said eventually. 'I assume you have chosen this campsite with the same astute care. May I ask what I might expect?'

'This camp has ass-toot care, does it?' Jek smirked back. Den caught that joke nice and quick, and he started chuckling with good cheer.

'Ass toot,' he snickered.

Pira humoured them with a smile and waited for an answer. 'Right,' Jek said. 'Well, tonight, my lady, our pleasure shall be visual instead of auditory.' He watched her eyes widen that he knew such words. You didn't need to be a simple man to enjoy a simple life.

'I see,' she said.

'You will,' Jek agreed. Den gave that a laugh as well. Great audience, was Den.

When the fades arrived, Pira let out a gasp of delight. The night was dark, but she was lit by firelight, and Jek could see the blossom of wonder spread across her face. Those fades were breathtaking alright – in every deadly way. The Swamp of Songs liked to hold on to the bodies, to preserve them as it would and make them scream or sing, but the Faded Forest took the souls. It meant the spirits continued on, after the swamp stopped their bodies short, and Jek assumed that these phantoms still believed they might one day make it to Lake Unknown. They didn't understand that they were now trapped within those trees. Appearing only at night, in a storm of blazing colour, the fades of the forest who couldn't step beyond the woods. That was what made the campsite so safe, since it had a solid clearing all around, and that was also what made the camp so sublime. Here, they could sit and admire and attempt to take in all of life's blinding light.

That was what Jek thought of it, anyway. He reckoned everyone's soul burned its own unique colour, each one fuelled by it in all directions, and that was why every fade was lit so distinctly brilliant. Maybe the one who shined that luminous pale green had been an artist. And maybe the one who sparkled dazzling silver had been a loving parent to their kids. It was the inner light of each and every soul who had walked into these woods and the beauty of it never failed to bring Jek and Den to tears. Not in sorrow that they had died, but at how magnificently they had lived.

As peaceful as these fades appeared to be, however, they were deadly to ever touch. The world only let you be one or the other. The living and the dead weren't meant to coexist. That was why the woods couldn't be walked at night, and why this clearing was so special. It was possible to rush through this entire stretch of forest in one day, but then you'd miss all of this. And it wasn't just the beauty those figures of light embodied. It was the sense of possibility that light implied. It was a glimpse of something larger, about the ultimate destiny of every life, and Jek was happiest to never fully understand it. It was enough to be this close. To feel a truth he couldn't see. Just like Den, Jek didn't have to get the entire joke.

It took time for Pira to pull her eyes away from the stunning sight. She was crying, just like Jek was, just like Den. She moved closer and placed her fingers around Jek's fists, to thank him for showing her this. He didn't know how he was supposed to respond.

'We don't sleep tonight,' he grunted. Pira turned back to make sure the fades weren't moving beyond the trees. Jek shook his head. 'Not them. It's the next stretch around the lake, the Cackling Plains, we can't travel there by day.'

Quite the trap, really. Not safe to travel the woods by night, and not sane to travel the plains by day.

'We stay awake,' he explained, 'and make a run through the last of the woods just before it's dark. It means a few crows might take a dive at us, but me and Den can handle them when it's just a few.' And not the swarms of hundreds they'd often seen blackening the skies. Even if the cackle crows were a normal size of bird – and they weren't – no one could fight off a hundred beaks and claws.

'A few crows?' Pira asked, although she had the sense not to sound too doubting.

'Even one is a fight,' Jek said.

'Even one is a fright!' Den laughed.

Jek joined him. 'What's the most of them we could fright, Den?'

Den had trouble answering through his fun. 'I could fright frive!'

'Frive!' Jek exclaimed. 'The most I could fright is frour!'

Den was laughing so much now he doubled over head-first into his brother. Jek wrapped his arms around him and they both shook with the same mirth. A damn beautiful man, was ugly old Den.

The timing was always delicate when they organised the transition from forest to plains, from day to night, but Jek and Den had years of practice and this one went as well as they could expect. They even had enough daylight left as they got to the edge of the Faded Forest that Pira could see the enormous carcass of a dead cackle crow. She thought it was the skeleton of a horse or deer.

'You think a horse or deer could make it in this far?' Jek asked. 'That there is a cackle crow. Or what's left of one, after the others ate it. Me and Den being such good guides and all, there isn't much else for them to eat. Damn giants have no choice but to turn on each other.'

Pira had nothing to say to that. Her eyes simply moved away from the dead behemoth and began to scan the skies. She wouldn't see anything up there. Cackle crows preferred to stay above the clouds until it was time to swoop. This close to the trees, anyway – further out on the empty plains, they flew as low as they chose. There was nowhere to hide from them out there, no way to run. They had eyes sharp enough to count the wispy hairs atop Den's balding head, but their hearing wasn't great, nor was their sense of smell. It meant they didn't hunt at night, or if they did, then they weren't half as good at it as they were by day. That was how Jek and Den got their clients across the final stretch of this quest. They walked slow and by night, and if they heard any cackling, they had their swords ready. It was probably the only part of the journey where Jek and Den couldn't laugh together. Damn birds laughed enough for them anyway.

One pleasing thing about it though, was that they were heading west. That, along with the flat horizon of the empty plains, made for an impressive sunset. The shimmer underneath that crimson sky with brush-strokes of gold made Den think he could see Lake Unknown from here. Jek didn't think so, since they couldn't see it at any other time of the day, but the best part of all beauty was that it showed every person their very own truth.

Once the sun had vanished, and before the light followed with it, Jek saw Pira turn and look at him, an expression of open admiration on her face. 'How many times have you experienced these wonders, Jek? Witnessed these sights? Does the feeling ever dull?'

Jek lifted his eyebrows at the woman that she could ask him such a question. Clearly she didn't understand the size of the things she spoke of if she thought their beauty could run out.

'I don't hear any cackling,' he said instead of scolding her. 'I reckon it's safe for us to go.'

'Safe for us to crow,' Den said quietly, but he knew better than to joke around now.

They spent the rest of that night silent, with swords drawn. The sky wasn't as dark as Jek would've liked, but it helped guide them on their way. Lake Unknown was large enough that they'd end up there no matter which way they walked, but it was always best not to spend too long on the plains. Hike around here at the wrong time of year and daybreak was on you before you'd made it halfway. Only reaching the lake could guarantee safety. Jek had seen those beasts drinking there before, but whatever magic powered it was enough to stop the crows attacking. Didn't make it easier being close to such wild creatures. Jek had tried to find their beauty beneath the cackling, but they hid it a little too deeply for even him to see.

The only sounds they heard that night were the gentle steps of their own boots. Den whispered that he could hear the lapping of the lake before Jek saw its reflection of the moon. Pira almost went foolish then, rushing ahead on instinct. Jek grabbed her arm to stop her, told her not to approach the water until it was dawn.

'Will you tell me about the lake now we're here, Jek?' Something about her lips parting to say his name made Jek feel all sorts of things he wished he didn't. It was extremely likely that this woman was about to die. Like everything else on this quest, there was its own form of beauty in that. Someone giving up their life to see the culmination of that life's goal. But Jek would rather hope that Pira was going to be one of the ones who made it.

'As soon as dawn arrives, Pira,' he said, his voice catching slightly as he said her name, 'you walk down to that lake and you look inside. Whatever is reflected back at you will be the answer to your question, the truth and beauty that drives each of us to dream. Your destiny will be close enough for you to touch, but it will be a doorway, not a picture. The same as the you from here can walk on in, the you from somewhere else can walk right out.'

Jek was expecting some reaction from her on hearing this, some manner of trepidation or surprise. All Pira did was nod, determined. She would face whatever she had to face. Den was quiet now. This was the only day of the trek that he didn't like. He understood that it was an important part, and that no single piece could define the whole, but he also didn't like to see things end.

'Sometimes,' Jek went on, 'no one comes out. But the ones here, looking in, they end up changed. Maybe their dreams weren't what they'd hoped, or maybe they weren't willing to pay its price. Whatever the reason, they're rarely the same people returning home. Something inside them dies. Something important, I think. Others, they die in the more traditional way.'

Pira's expression tightened at this, as if she knew what she would hear. Jek narrowed his eyes at the unusual woman. He finished telling her all he knew. 'The other them, the ones from their destiny, they challenge. They attack. And they usually win. Only very few, the ones who want this bad enough, they fight to the death for their dreams, and they're the ones who live. They might be barely standing from that battle, but they stand victorious, and they enter the lake to claim their prize. I don't know where they go. All I know is that they don't come back.'

There was more that Jek could say. He could tell her about the ones who faced no challenge. Who simply saw what they desired and took it. But he wanted her to know the risk. He wanted her to live.

'Did you ever look into Lake Unknown, Jek?'

He breathed in deeply through his nose and thought about a lie. Her gaze was just too piercing though, her expression too intent.

'I did,' he admitted. And, apart from Den, she was probably the only person in the world he'd ever told. He waited for the next question to arrive. For her to ask him what he saw. For her to ask him what happened then. But she seemed happy with his answer, as if some truth or beauty about him had just been confirmed.

When the sun stretched up above the lake, the body of water opened up to fill forever. A small herd of cackle crows could be seen on a far shore. Their enormous size played tricks with distance, so Jek couldn't be sure how far they were away. Close enough for the eyes of the vicious creatures to all focus on the three humans on the other side. The beasts cackled at them, sending ripples across the lake, and they went back to drinking their fill.

Pira's confidence had not faltered upon seeing the monsters. She had eyes now only for the lake. She stepped forward to meet her fate, but before she did, she turned briefly to smile at Jek and Den. 'Thank you,' she said. 'For getting me this far. Now I must do the rest myself.'

As she walked down to the shore, Pira unwrapped her robes. The strips of bright cloth fell to the ground like sunshine. The painted flesh beneath looked like night. All over her naked body were designs and spirals of purple and blue, cut into her skin with the kind of detail that could only have taken decades to create. Suddenly Jek knew that no guardian would step out to challenge Pira. She had spent her life already fighting them and had defeated every one.

At the edge of the lake, Pira halted just before her toes touched the water. For the longest time she stared down at its surface, enthralled by what she could see. Part of Jek wanted her to turn away, but more of him wanted her to fulfil her dream. When she did turn, it was just her head, and it was to smile at Jek.

'I wish I could share this with you,' she said. 'You've shared so much with me.'

'I appreciate the invitation,' he said back, 'but I'm happy where I am.'

She smiled that mysterious smile of hers again. 'When you looked into the lake, Jek. What did you see?'

Jek scratched his jaw and thought why not. He'd never see her again. And, truth be told, he wanted her to know. So, he wrapped an arm around his brother, and they gifted her with a laugh.

'I saw this. I saw me and Den, laughing together, making the most of our life, no matter where we were.'

'So you never needed to make the journey,' she said. 'You were already there…' And, suddenly, she was laughing too. 'That's beautiful,' she whispered, and then she walked into the lake.

AISLING

Danny Brennan

The kitchen cabinets are glowing. I can see through them to their stacked porcelain guts. Everything dims as my head drops. Shit.

The kitchen resurfaces from the purpling darkness. I am on the floor eye to eye with a loose chickpea. I check for matted blood in my hair and find just matted hair. I get up slowly, scanning for fractures. Turning the cold tap, I grab a glass from the now solid kitchen press. I've not fainted in years. Since mass – the smell of frankincense and wet school jumpers. In the dark kitchen window my spectral reflection judges me. Oversized tee shirt. Shitty flannel PJ bottoms. Ginger hair all over the place. Swaying. Eyeliner migrating across my face. I'm still drunk and maybe more. Standing in the freezing kitchen looking into my glass of water like I am on a diving board. The house fills the glass. I am above my bed. The duvet slowly rises and falls. There's somebody in there. Who owns that body?

Fuck, so the night before I was in Sweeneys' Lane. A cobbled in-between place where people too young or too weird to get into proper pubs go. The vibe is – this is where you can find drugs. That's why I was there. I'd been at an exhibition where the artist had filled glass dinosaur bones with crude oil and assembled them into skeletons. It was sponsored by Google so there was an open whiskey bar. People stood around and congratulated the artist on their social conscience. I alienated the two girls from college by getting too drunk, and loudly shit talking corporate sponsorship within earshot of the artist. Sineád and Saoirse thought of their career trajectory in the arts and ditched me, giving one of those tiny little waves from across the room,

Bye Aisling.

I ended up talking to the curator. Straight fringe down to her eyes and black culottes. She had a little freckle on her cheek and wine stains on her berry rose lipstick. We argued about corporate sponsorship, art washing and whether political art could change anything, then at some point I started showing her pictures of my artwork. I had made a tiny slide for a projector from a series of sonograms that I stole from my mum and then overlaid with cracks in the pavement and spiderwebs. She feigned interest very well. She was a very good curator. She touched my elbow and the alcohol in my blood evaporated. She leaned in close and said,

Would you be able to sort us out?

This was predictable but I had wanted to be surprised. I caught myself and smiled.

What can I do for you? I bring my hand to my chin.

Oh you know, whatever, she dismissed it as an afterthought.

She wanted coke. I made some noncommittal sounds about maybe knowing someone. We swapped numbers. I said I would let her know.

She walked into the crowd. I lost sight of her because every-one was wearing black. Everyone including me was wearing black. They wouldn't give me another drink at the supposedly open bar. Some streak of shit in a black polo neck and a bucket hat walked up to me and asked if I had ever been to Berlin. I handed him my empty glass and walked out of the room. I rolled a cigarette on the way out the door. I smoked instead of screaming. The smoke eased the tension headache that threat-ened to close my nose piercing and also kill me. I cut across the city to the lane smoking my rollie to the nub – flicking embers into the night.

In the windowed alcove in the kitchen, I ball up on the chair. We've been in this squat three months. The train shakes us awake at 6:30 in the morning. We built this table from pal-lets and the ashtray is made from an old beer can folded like origami. I scavenge for cigarette butts and find a half-smoked joint. I spark up and get an afterglow – a flash of tumbling and pulsing ferment in the air. Staring at the end of the joint, I see past it and through the peephole out the front door. Through the cones of streetlights. The Earth spins up to meet me. I see through the water pipes. Down past the strata of Viking then Iron Age Dublin. I see through the boiling mantle of the Earth. It is all clear as air. I see the serpentine course of my life, it stretches before me like a map of a cave system in blown glass. I can see myself, legs dangling at a café and a huge cup of cof-fee in front of me. My mum looked over the steam of her cup telling me about her day. I reach for the mug. Hot coffee kisses my bare legs. I snap back to myself. I'm definitely still on something.

I strolled up to the lane and the crowd looked like they were tearing each other apart. This was good. If the lane was quiet it meant something terrible was about to happen. I got a wave from a few of the old heads. Ger started chatting the ear off me. He'd be about 15, I think, and wore a suit too big for him. His sandy hair nearly matched his sallow skin. He had brothers, bad men that moved weight. A sweet boy though. He offered me a key of coke. I turned him down. He patted his suit pocket and pulled out another baggie – yellow and chalky.

'Bump of speed,' he smiled at his magic trick. I shrugged and took the car key and the bag he offered. I spoke to fellow session gremlins as their heads bobbed to the drum and bass that leaked up from the cellar. Aaron was having words with a young lad who was selling drugs above the market rate. Aaron always had a knife on him and Dagan, his older brother, was not here to tell him to go butter toast. Last week Dagan had fought two men while balls naked. The guards had to wait till he finished a rollie before he let them cuff him.

I got chatting to a few fresh-faced tourists who were looking for squalor. Clad in hiking gear. Drinking pints of Guinness with straws sticking out of them. I refused to give them the satisfaction of saying anything. The guy had the intelligence of a mercenary and tried to talk to me about Irish politics. His girlfriend or sister who had escaped from a Terrence Malick film was all messy hair and golden hours. I took her hand and brought her down the narrow stairs to dance. The room was packed. The walls were wet with sweat. The DJ's tongue was lodged in his nose as he tried to hold the world together. Dropping Amen break after Amen break to this temporary cargo cult. Me and the blonde girl danced defensively until we pushed through the layer of handsy lurkers and got in front of the speakers, where people were actually dancing. The speakers rippled through the air in our lungs. Echoed down through all our past selves right back through the million years that we have danced around the fire. We danced till we were sore. I tasted phlegm and iron at the back of my throat. We grabbed a glass of water at the bar and dragged each other back up the stairs. The boyfriend/brother was annoyed about something and the two of them started to bicker so I left them to it. I fell back into the crowd. I got chatting to a really tall hippie. He was pushing 7 feet. He smelled of patchouli and he affected the wind speed in the lane. Apparently he was the shortest of seven brothers. We leaned against the brick wall held up by layers of graffiti. I used the curl of my fingers to guard the joint as he did a spread. Then he placed a piece of rice cracker wrapped in cling film in my hand. He smiled and walked into the night, sparking his joint. Fucking hippies. The rice cake had mass to it. I had some bad times on acid. Devour yourself starting with your feet till you disappear sort of bad. I was trying to find my better judgement when I saw Mer looking at me across the crowd. She wore a little mustard beanie and turned all the light that touched her purple. As I walked over she turned away from me. I had not seen her for a while. After she got glassed and lost her eye, she and I went on a screaming bender. She was angry. She wanted to die. She wanted revenge. She lacked depth perception. We spent a lot of time shoulder to shoulder, carrying each other in and out of bars. Counting how many guys would walk over then turn and run as soon as they saw her eye patch and the shatter pattern scars. She avoided me after that.

The rice cake dissolved on our tongues like a communion wafer. We danced around each other. Pretence burned away.

I can't believe this is happening again, Mer said to me. I turned to look at her. What did she mean again?

This is what happens every fucking time. It's like you go out of your way to fuck me up. I'm looking at my hands at the slow flushing of the blood vessels.

I never meant to.

No? You're like the crossroad I go to sell my soul at. Then I wonder why I am hanging out alone in the dark.

What do you mean?

You're only ever trying to help yourself.

Why did you decide to trip with me if you think I'm so bad?

Because I'm pissed. She smiled with a kind razor sadness.

The space between us filled with bodies. People chatted loud and clutched pints. Eyes became more prominent. The poisoning of alcohol became clear as people sloshed around us like they had eaten the wrong berries. I began to see subtle changes of colour in faces as people breathed in and out. The whole lane began to breathe in and expand and pulse like the intestine of a beast. I was standing beside Mer again. It had either been a few minutes or many aeons. I was tracing out my life in the mortar between the brickwork. Afraid to look at her. Mer was glowering. I reached out to her and traced the button holes of her coat. Then I kissed her and for a moment she kissed me. She whipped her head back.

Are you only into girls when you're high?

No this is real.

You said that before.

Behind her, in the gaps between the brickwork, the nights before played out like a Willow pattern had come to life. I downed shots with Mer and then left her to dance alone. Mer passed out at a table holding my coat. I pulled boys into corners. She would get annoyed. I'd kiss her neck. Then when she called me out, I told her she was straight. I told her I was straight. I told her she was taking advantage of me. I told her about what happened to me. So drunk – my eyes could not look to see. The next time I would pretend none of it happened. Again and again.

Sat on a bed. My shoes are downstairs. My socks don't match. Water and steam creep from under the door.

Mer held me. I said I am sorry, in slow descending circles. Mer cooed and whispered sweetnesses. Through the gaps in the bricks, I saw the glass skeleton of my memories laid out for forensics. The same spiderweb fractures suffuse my life. I saw my mum running around trying to do everything to distract herself from what was happening. Stitched herself to my father. Her grey eyes looked at me and willed everything to be okay but she could not look to see.

Mer had brought me away from the lane, the crowds, and the cracks in the walls that stared back at me. I think I was mute as I looked at the crystalline echoes of my life. The same vibration through different bones. Mer rolled me a rollie. Put it in my hand. On the boardwalk I was standing looking at the dark flowing waters of the Liffey, so many of its tributaries buried underground. The sodium orange streetlights, the muddy brown of dark windows and the silver of the moon made purple and Mer looked at me, her working eye tilted towards me. She lit my cigarette. It felt like smoking nothing at all.

I've been thinking, Mer said. I need to stop this. I know you have your own shit to deal with but I don't think you know a single thing about me.

Tell me, I said. It was all I could manage.

Mer put her coat around my shook body and we walked towards my home.

She spoke quickly, her lips close together, conducting her thoughts with her hands. She wanted to study film. She told me she loved Jane Campion, Terrence Malick, the Coen Brothers, Steve McQueen and Sally Potter. I told her I had watched the *Tree of Life* after she had suggested it. I just said, Wow. Fuck. She nodded sagely. I had no idea what time it was. The streets were calm but for a quiet thrum and the yellow lights of taxis. Mer told me about her parents. They were loving. Religious. They wanted her to do well. They worked all the time, both in healthcare. She could go out late as long as she got back in time for school. They wanted her to do a profession. Anything but a doctor. She said she was staying over at a friend's house. They have been strict since the attack. She had to lie more. I didn't know she was eighteen. We got back to my house. She looked up at the looming tower block of the Google corporation that put my house in the shade. My housemates were sleeping or still out. We snuck slowly upstairs, careful of each creaking board. I wrapped myself in a duvet and lay down on the floor. Mer sat on the bed clicking her boots together.

I sit here the sun colouring the sky lilac grey. Ben comes down early, as always. He looks at me through his sleep-filled eyes and blond and messy hair. He chooses not to engage me in a conversation about conspiracy theories but puts the kettle on and efficiently rolls me a joint. The tea is perfectly bitter like the earth. I turn down the joint. A few hours later I can talk again. Mer comes down the stairs two at a time. She doesn't even look back as she flies out the door.

TANK

Aria K. C.

If I reminded you of all the rot kids get up to when there are no parents around, you wouldn't believe me. You wouldn't want to.

Remember the back heel crunch spattering fever-green snot across tarmac? The eviction of insects (for many their first experience as the future landlords they grew up to become) from their nests and subsequent penknife amputations?

All sorts of awful nonsense. You couldn't handle the best of it, trust me. I don't want to believe it myself most of the time. Of course, then, I must reflect on my place, on my duty to remain an impartial observer.

I was employed as a full-time biographer. It was my mission to produce a complete and legible account on my chosen subject's life.

Forgive me, *chosen* is not the right word. I was not given a choice.

The subject *assigned* to me was an individual born on the 5th day of March, 1998, in the University Galway Hospital while the tail-end of a storm, dubbed Georgia, swept across the Atlantic to harass the city for the night.

It must be stated clearly, the newborn more than likely lured that blustery blather to begin with, my working theory being, dysphoric babies attract stormy weather.

Similar to my lack of say in the matter, they were assigned male at birth, a fact they would later come to discover was not a fact at all but a grave joke and one that was sufficiently terrible enough to land minus a punchline. Bestowed Georgia Lannan, a number of convoluted reasons later prevented them from seeing their birth cert and only George was used. Lovingly upon the temple, a battery acid kiss of love and nonsensical cooing, labelled early animal speak, was the wax seal on another bitter joke.

I acted as observer. I took notes. Occasionally, when the numerals and glyphs aligned, I pretended I knew what it all meant. I never once interfered with ill intent or to redirect them onto another path. What they chose to think, say and do was entirely of their own volition.

The problem is, I don't want to share all the sordid little details and gruesome acts I accumulated over the years, I couldn't do it. Not even the softest twilight connivance.

What I do want to tell you about is a pivotal and tumultuous event that I... I mean that the subject of my extensive research found themselves entangled in.

It was summer.

No, my apologies; it was the idea of summer. Still three weeks away and during the counting down of days until the last school bell, George found themselves afoul lonely walks in warm, slanted evening rain. From an early age they relished hiding in their room, divining accepted forms of astral projection. If they ever stole away to a mirror, bra nervously clutched, I wouldn't know about it. Trust me; I wasn't in on any of it.

The first time they confided in me, I did not respond. I feared spoiling my vantage point, but let me tell you, I felt validated. This is a lonely occupation; a lonely world to find yourself the expendable piece.

Where was I?

It was the thought of summer. The breeze carried faint music from nearby estates George had not yet visited, as a result, the noise of play, of childish vaunting which I have no reservations in describing as water squeezing concentrated out the funnel's tip, blended into the background. Kerbside in their pensive reverie, George was want for something to do, when the world decided to sink two metres. Dull as the road-weeds that do not flower but seem to flourish to a state of hardy banality; puberty came on rapidly. They fell clean off the kerb. Knees scuffed. A tick stretched across the grey stone with a fingertip.

Over the course of the next three weeks George realised they were born with the incorrect set of bomb disposal equipment. Testosterone-led changes trapped them. First showings of hair, first carnal dreams, first gut wrenching attacks of fight or fight or fight…

It was summer. Truly. Long sleepless fits in delicate dark, an open window to trick the gentle cool of star soaked milk into the room. No school for two months. When they returned,

George would be entering secondary school, Coláiste Éinde on Threadneedle Road if their sitting of the entrance exams proved adequate.

George was afraid of sitting idle too long after a television programme claimed that this fuelled growth spurts. Their bony skeleton was getting stretched further by the day. At one point I was quite afraid the ceiling would prove inadequate in height as lampshades were becoming a nuisance, doorways too.

I'm sorry, I'm dragging.

You want to know what the bad thing is, don't you? You won't have bothered to read this far if you don't believe I'm going to say it – if you don't think I'll spill the beans.

I will.

A biographer should never withhold, tamper with or misquote the truth. It is a sacred thing. I only wish to make clear that I will not tell you any lies. This should perhaps be taken as a warning.

George was a split teabag, granulated and fighting for breath in the cup. After lunch, we wandered the estate in search of something we had never seen before. That was the hope. There was a trio of prowling boys and in that carefree childhood way of recruiting every living soul in the vicinity to participate in one play-land, they introduced themselves, (I'll give them the cutely crafted anonymity of an abbreviation), as J, M, and R.

'What part of the estate do you live in,' J quizzed.

'The first part,' George answered and pointed to his right, to the row of houses facing them at the base of the hill. The estate was constructed in the shape of three side-by-side, interlocking Os. Ours nestled against the curve of a back wall that at the time contained the ongoing construction of a new estate.

'That's not the first part, that's the third part,' R said matter-of-factly. He pointed to his left, 'We live over there. That's the first part.'

M crossed his arms as if George's response might require a firm change of belief. His hair was a short slick of hair gel, an organism the way it glistened. He wore a red rubber and plastic watch, the face of which had been scraped with something sharp so as to render it useless.

'If I lived there, I would think it was the first part too.'

'Are you calling us liars?' R said.

'Yeah, are you?' M piped in.

'I think we're all correct to feel we live in the first part,' George chanced, unsure if the correct solution had been formulated.

M looked to R for how to proceed. R looked at J. George in turn looked at the scratched watch, perplexed.

I looked at the watch, equally puzzled.

Something about time startled us in that moment. Not the passing of time precisely, but the reminder it existed, that similar to M's hair, time lived and breathed and just like his watch, it was easy to miss. It threw us into a state of play-pretend and George tried an interpretation of a reasonable male, little stare off into the far distance – cutting moss off a stone with formulaic iciness. I intervened and gave George a little nudge.

Now, I know what you're going to say, '*What about when you said a biographer should never intervene?*'

Well, I did. You probably want me to confess a sense of pride in helping, but if I'm being honest, it was purely about survival.

'I can tell, you're only kidding aren't you?' R said.

'Course.'

A seven-week relationship was established on the basis of my suave tongue.

It was all surface level; the conversation that is. I never managed to glean a single reliable piece of information, as if the kid's realities changed with each passing hour.

If I knew then what was to come, would I have intervened? Even though it is the role of the biographer to remain omnipotent, a ghostly shroud on the overlooked side of your burnt toast, I like to think I would be consistent.

A bike ramp was stodgily crafted for the benefit of J's younger brother to wipe the front row of his teeth out – loose pebbledash the way they scattered. Games like Bomb on The Road which was really a brick, or Brick on The Road, which was really a mineral-bomb to the car's axles. My favourite was The Invisible Rope Trick: an elegantly simple jest wherein two people, very seriously I might add, took either end of an imaginary string and pulling it taut, stood on opposite sides of the road. The oncoming car would jerk to a stop in fear of damage to the vehicle, a smash of brass.

I'm sure it never crossed the kid's minds that the drivers might have been afraid of damaging *them*.

Several weeks passed in such a way that George failed to notice even the mundane connective tissue that held the days together; sleeping, eating, washing. It was I who carried the burden of appearances and who dutifully pulled through on the conversational end. I produced the correct noises when required, when pressed. When there was absolutely no other choice, I ran with the role and built George a little thicker of mud; lies to please. I helped create an invented depth of character, something a tad more substantial than a repressed thread of elastic, so that when J, M and R offered for George to venture with them on a capping spree, I happily went in their place.

Capping, as was soon explained, involved scouting for and stealing valve-caps from the tyres of cars. None of the black rubber or plastic ones though. The fruit's sole requirement for picking was it had to be made of metal. J, M, and R each possessed vast collections they had gathered since the prior weekend; when J first heard about capping from his older cousin at a family barbecue. As they weren't afraid to venture farther distances in search of better crops, they had not only exhausted the local supply but had capped as far as Salthill.

I never got to pick a single cap, not that day or any other. If vehicles of any kind existed where I am now, I would be tempted to look.

Unable to find anymore, J, M and R soon grew bored, consequently that meant I had to feign my own apathy about the valve-caps.

Next, it was all about setting fire to the dried gorse in the abandoned field and stealing just enough drink so parents wouldn't find out. A game of patience. The boys would show up with a beer or can of cider apiece, whereas George would create a cocktail of apocalyptic design, namely: fruit concentrate, white wine, red wine, cider and any other spirit that was lying about.

Sorry, I said I wouldn't get into the really messy bits, didn't I?

Another two weeks came and passed like the penetrating stare of a passenger seat cancer victim. Summer was ending. The days were still long and glorious but the window returned to a sealed position as the nights grew steadily colder.

There is a day that falls annually in the middle of August with the potential to be referred to as the last nice day of the year. It was that morning, a Wednesday, as it happened. George and I were embroiled in harnessing the power of the sun to burn holes in the sleeves of an old jumper. In the process of ushering George onward in the journey of fire, I planted in their mind the idea to focus the sun's intensity onto their skin, perhaps the top of the hand and that way the scar could be from anything…

J and M came bounding over the Council-designated play-space, a well managed green pen, quick on the upturn of the ankle to send airborne Council-cut grass. Summers hot speckle in their cheeks saw them flushed.

'You'll never believe what R found,' M said, panting.

'What?'

'Words are no good,' J said, mystifying further.

'But what is it?'

'Come see for yourself. He's at the tank.'

We trooped over to the tank – a large metal box mid-way between the estate's three Os which hummed with the constant spirit of electricity. A perimeter wall constructed around the green container meant that a cosy hideout existed for those who could climb their way up and drop down into the staple-shaped gap between wall and tank. It was the designated spot to urinate when too far from home, although its efficiency came with the added risk somebody might climb up and catch you in the act.

I asked George one night, why they referred to it as the tank; however, they had no memory of any christening. They were adamant it had nothing to do with storage and very little to do vehicles.

'What is it then?' George asked.

J and M sniggered.

M rapped on the front face of the metal, his knuckles striking the ESB logo concealed beneath a cacophonic swirl of meandering spray-paint. 'George's here,' he said, raising the volume of his voice.

A reply was hurled out of the interior gap, 'Give me a minute.'

We stood in silence, steeped in it. By the time I figured out something to say, J had hopped out of the gap. He stood beside us, lips twisted at an odd angle, a stupid grin on his face.

'You aren't going to believe what I found,' he said.

Reaching around, he lifted the back of his shirt and produced a rolled magazine from his waistband.

'We're going to be rich,' he beamed beatifically.

Unfurled with great care, the black and white cover depicted a semi-nude female figure. Her scanner-toned, naturally curly hair framed a soft, yet, photographically pronounced face; eyes outlined with an unidentifiable colour across the lids. She had an expression that said, us, the audience, had done something terrible but there weren't going to be any punishments as the photo was not realistic enough to conjure such depths.

'I thought porn was supposed to be in colour,' M speculated.

George was enamoured. The others too. Not for the same reasons, I soon discovered.

The magazine, titled *Gal*, was intended for a bisexual audience. On the margin of the first page, below an editorial staff of clearly false names, the descriptor "*Printed in Connemara*" could be read. It featured male models the boys would skip amid groans of dissatisfaction, apart from R. He met George's wandering stare, a beacon of glimmering radio signals. Androgynous models were likewise skipped. J was the finder, the keeper and therefore the controller of the illicit material. His personal preferences dictated what were deemed the "correct" draws and triggers. A flick through, with ample time spent on each female model, revealed the trio's questionable opinions. Generous perusal was even paid to the dull, flame-singeing pages of black text and the advertisements proclaiming a guaranteed safe method of enlarging one's member. The postal box where the twenty euro was to be sent listed the address as Waterford, the recipient, Ms. Reardon Peen.

The plan was un-diabolically simple: the magazine would be rented in ten minute slots at the cost of two euro.

'How will you track the ten minutes?' George asked.

'M has a watch, keep up.'

The problem came when J suggested the offending male and androgynous pages be torn out and destroyed as only the pictures of women were of worth. He revealed he had already done so with a particularly off-putting image and refused to elaborate further. R argued that because it catered to more than one type of person, they could use this to their advantage and double their profits.

After much deliberation and an uncomfortable lathering of pointed rhetoric, it was decided that no pages were to be torn out.

Before parting, J made us climb into the concealed staple-shaped gap with him. Moving a broken panel of jagged plywood, he revealed his gift to us: a centrefold poster carefully duct taped to the tank. A woman posing with her weight rested on one side, hip angled away from the rest of her body.

'Just for us,' he declared proudly.

I watched George try and fail miserably to re-create the same pose a few hours later. They stood in front of the bathroom mirror while I watched from the unfilled bathtub, trying and failing, in my own way, at not making noise. Even my breathing, further reminder of how close I was, was enough to set George off at times.

'You know you have control over whether or not you stick around,' I prodded, biting my thumb to quell the snigger.

I couldn't help myself. The boys had kindled a bonfire of confidence in me.

'Why are you still here?' George asked dryly, refusing to look over.

'I'm your biographer. I am always here,' I replied. 'Besides, you haven't openly asked me to leave. *Ever.*'

'I have, plenty of times.'

'Not to my face.'

'I shouldn't have to say it to your face,' George pointed out. 'If you are an extension of me, anything I say to myself, you should be aware of. It shouldn't matter if I say it aloud or not.'

'I'm afraid it doesn't work like that.'

'What would you know about the way things work or don't work? You're only a biographer.'

'At least I know who I am,' I said.

George sighed and continued to ignore me. They pouted, gently tilting their head before scrambling their face in annoyance and relaxing their expression.

George mumbled, 'I guess that's why you're always trying to insert your opinion where it's not needed,' before going on to ask, 'Suppose I do tell you to leave, how can I be sure you won't come back unannounced, or worse, uninvited?'

'I'm sure they'll set me up with a retirement package, a bursary or a residency of some sort.'

'A *residency*? You've only chronicled thirteen years and for the majority of those you weren't even doing a good job. Why don't I remember my third birthday?'

'I'll admit I haven't been very clued-in to what you've been going through recently, but your third birthday had extensive analysis,' I said. 'Those were my golden years.'

I thought about my prior statement, my self-assured assumption there would be someone to look after me if George abandoned me, which is to say, George thought about it. After all, it was George who had to suffer through wanting so desperately to be alive and correct and at the same time, pleading for the encroach of death to pick up the pace, or at least act like it was less than ambivalent in the matter of their case.

'If you do tell me to leave, *where* will I go?'

We finally made eye contact. It was bathroom-tiles-and-blue-toothpaste-volatile, the two of us confined in that space.

'For a start, you can step outside. I need to pee,' George said blandly.

I lay awake the entire night fretting about my future, what abysmal residues were to linger. George had never asked me to leave a room before; if they moved to a new point in space, I was always by their side. I could feel it was the start of something much bigger and it frightened me immensely. I figured as long as I was able to access a desk, the good sturdy kind, adequate space for my knees to safely tuck underneath while I unearthed opulent fossils from the depths of the blank page's stratum, and pen and paper, enumerable quantities, I might be okay.

Somewhere to sleep would not go amiss either.

Blanket was optional, pillow was not.

The next morning I felt a bag of nerves. As part of the business arrangement, we had to keep watch while customers availed of the magazine in the privacy of the staple-shaped gap. George wasn't happy to be picked for security based on how intimidated one might feel with their height, but seeing as parents never walked anywhere and the older teenagers had moved on to more advanced pastimes, it was far from demanding work. A few young boys under the age of ten but they were shooed with little pressure.

It was R and George, kerbside.

R fidgeted with the top of his socks, green and grey stripes peeking out from the tops of his runners. His legs were still smooth and free of dark hair.

'So, I've been thinking,' he began. 'If we aren't going to get paid for this, the least J can do is let us use the magazine too, right?'

Experiencing a minor pang of envy, George sounded uninterested, 'I guess so.'

'What's wrong with you?'

'I'm not sure…'

I stepped in immediately.

'Nothing's wrong,' I said.

Thankfully J appeared around the corner, hands in pockets, whistling the sprite of his midday lunch.

'How's business?' he asked when close enough.

R, fulfilling his role as cashier, dropped a single coin into J's palm. J's smile quickly vanished.

'What's this? It costs two euro to use the magazine, this is only a euro.'

'Oh yeah, that was M. His mum wanted him home, so he said he would give us the other euro tomorrow.'

'Did he at least stick to ten minutes?'

R looked at George for assistance but soon saw there was none on offer. '*Umm*, I'm not really sure actually,' he answered with a nervous hesitancy. 'You see, M was wearing the watch so…'

'And *nobody* else has wanted to use it?'

We nodded solemnly.

J groaned, joining us on the kerb. 'I was sure this was going to make us some money.'

'There's always tomorrow,' R suggested hopefully.

'Where's the magazine now?'

There was a pause.

'I have it,' R said.

'Keep it for tonight,' J instructed. 'Throw it back to me–'

R jumped to his feet, 'Really? Thank you so much.'

He sped off in an excited blur.

George looked as if they weren't aware they had the ability to communicate outside of blinking. Sensing the possible awkwardness, I was once again about to intervene when J stood up.

'I'm going home,' he mumbled indifferently, more to himself than to George.

George didn't say goodbye. In solidarity, I remained quiet. We sat there a long time, kerbside, the sun bemoaning its gradual descent, sending forth an expulsion of light so as to rake the sky with streaks of apricot, farrows of citrusy weeping that stretched as far as the eye's limit.

'If we search, we can find someone who can help us,' I tried. 'We can restart. Me and you. We just need to remember there's a slight criminal element, we need to keep it where the knees go, if you catch my drift; all very under the desk.'

'Do whatever you want.'

'You have to give me something to work with George,' I pleaded. 'You're killing me here.'

'My name isn't George, your name is George. And yes, that's the idea.'

'What would you like me to call you?' I asked earnestly, hoping I could somehow change their mind, or that, if I stalled for long enough we might stumble upon some wonderful and clever means in which I might remain as their biographer, after all; I must agree I see absolutely no sense in Subject A being assigned to Biographer B when Subject A feels Biographer B is actually an electrician who fell from the wrong ceiling vent and is only taking initiative from the electrician who instructed them on how best to react if ever they found themselves cruelly ejected from the heights of a metal aperture. On the other hand, I did not want to be out of a job.

What I'm trying to say is, I no longer represented my assigned subject's best interests and it unsettled me.

'Call me Sophronia.'

'*Sophronia?*'

'Actually, now I've heard you say it, scrap that. Call me Jane.'

'Agreed. Jane definitely suits you more,'

Jane smiled. Getting to her feet, she approached the green tank. Once at the top, she dropped inside the gap.

I dutifully followed.

Cramped. Stench of urine frosting. A mature cider sugar factory and something buried in the corner. Living and breathing time, shades of deep space corpus.

Jane pulled the jagged plyboard away from the side of the tank; the taped poster of the model she tried to emulate was still there. As the only picture hanging in the estate's private gallery, an air of pride surrounded it. She patiently loosened the corners of the tape with her nails. Once a tantalising lip had lifted, I watched her carefully work the sides so as not to tear the image, all the way around, in a restrained display of the wrist, until it peeled free.

'What are you planning on doing with it?' I questioned.

'Study material,' Jane said, chuffed with her handiwork.

Holding the poster in front of her, the thin, cheap paper was penetrated by illumination from above. The image on the reverse side began to peek through. I was shoulder to shoulder with Jane, and we spotted it at the same time. She flipped the poster.

The first transgender person I had ever seen.

The first transgender person *Jane* had ever seen.

It was a revelation. Her world was roughly tussled, shook by pneumatic hands that despised the presence of dirt as if the fabric of her life was a dust laden carpet.

This wasn't like any throwaway scene from a television show or a movie where Hollywood's hottest action star is convinced by their agent to don a wig and show how versatile their acting chops are; this was an actual trans body.

Her hair, clipped at the back, allowed certain strands to fall just so. She had a vague accent of broad shoulders Jane found gorgeous. Petite breasts, the kind, she added, she would happily settle for, slip-the-slide-down smooth skin, hips and a cute backside, all the way down to her quaint genitals which were dainty in appearance.

Jane was enamoured, practically ecstatic.

I was once again frightened, my existence rapidly fleeting right in front of me. There was no other choice left but to confront it head on.

'Do you reckon everybody started calling this the tank because it's full of electric fish?' I asked, both intent on changing the subject and suffering no change in my assigned subject.

'I want to look like her,' Jane said.

'Yes, well you look like me, so you can't.'

'If she can do it, so can I. Besides, it's not entirely about looks, it's about who's telling my story. Take the day I tried to pose like the woman from this poster. I guarantee you described me as "trying" and "failing."'

'*I* was assigned as the biographer, not you. I think I know how to do my job, thank you very much!'

Lips pursed, Jane stuck the poster to the front of her t-shirt so as to free both hands in aid of an efficient escape. Standing at the top, she turned to face me. I felt a reduction of my former self among flaxen tumours.

'I refuse to give you my consent to chronicle my life anymore,' Jane declared. 'You're fired, or retired or banished, or whatever happens to biographers when they're no longer wanted.'

I watched her leave, slack-jawed but knowing in my heart it was for the best.

You may ask, '*What does happen to biographers after their talents are no longer required?*'

I stayed on in the staple-shaped gap of the tank for a stint, nourished by the estate's tumours. Curiously, I believe the layers of rubbish in the gap helped stem the pull but at some point, things started to breakdown. Dagger jolts of electricity seized my body, a sensation of being sucked into the mantle of the Earth. Then, the light refused to settle in any coherent manner my retinas could effectively translate, until a sudden, bellicose bang cleared my ears and I was removed, quite literally, out of the picture.

I live between worlds now, a figment of biological mistruth that never really existed. I am not flesh. I am not blood. I am not any of those gruesome or divine liquids at the heart of the world's ceremonies.

I cannot say much more.

I have this much of a tale to tell; my life was short and none the worse for it, I tell you this honestly. It wasn't really a life if you ask me or Jane for that matter, not the way it was headed. I live in a pillowless room with a stupefying view now (don't ask me what of, I am forbidden to say) with a decent sized desk to safely accommodate my writing and my knees.

The blanket's not much to write about. I feel it tabulating at night.

Convinced the new biographer will be coming any day, I have recently been filling-in the blanks. When they pick up where I've left off all will be neat and in order.

My only hope is that my successor finds out why the kids called it the tank.

AND FINDING ONLY SONGS WE'VE SUNG

Tom Javoroski

The chairs were cold underneath his legs. He tried a second, and a third, to the same effect. Though they were upholstered and cushioned and surprisingly comfortable, and though he wore heavy cotton pants, they reminded him of plastic waiting-room chairs. *Like in a dentist's office*, he thought. *Or a pharmacy.* Those plastic chairs. Always cold.

The third chair was back next to her, on her right now. He almost turned to look at her fully, but she was reading a magazine, picked up from the low table in front of them.

'Are these chairs cold?'

The magazine had her. 'No.'

'Hmm.' He looked around the room again, trying to avoid the painting on the opposite wall. It was hideous – so much colour, but so barren a soul. He had many like it stacked in his garage.

'They feel cold, to me. You know... like plastic ones.'

'Mmm.'

The magazine was about hunting. Or birds. Other issues were fanned out before them on the table, containing articles on canoeing, training your hunting dog, and choosing the right hip waders. He would have laid money that she had never seen hip waders, in the flesh. He never had.

Ten minutes later, he'd learned more about hunting dog training tips than in the whole of his life to that moment. And he'd only really read two of them. But she was still reading, so he read.

Impersonal interests, he said to himself. *They're good for you. Hunting dogs will never affect my life.*

The door to the inner office opened, and they both set their magazines down. They were the only ones in the waiting room – the door could only be opening for them.

'Hector,' the man said, 'Eve. We're all set.'

His lab coat preceded them down a short, well-lit hallway, past unmarked doors and corner niches filled with uncluttered desks. Hector wasn't sure he trusted anyone with an uncluttered desk. The three people they passed in the hallway, however, were all lab-coated and nodding politely, and so he belayed his suspicions. *These desks are for show. Or reception.*

Eve reached down between them as they walked, took his hand. He started, squeezed. She squeezed back.

They found the clutter when they passed through another seemingly inconspicuous door. The room beyond contained only one desk, but four separate bookshelves, each overflowing with volumes and loose papers. A large whiteboard occupied one wall – it was blank, but with signs of use, black and red shadows like when words used to burn into his father's TVs – and a door stood open opposite the one they came in.

Behind the desk was the woman they knew. The one they trusted. Dressed in a superhero fandom sweatshirt and jeans, she stood up, shook their hands, and waved the other man out. She read Hector's mind as she gestured they should follow her through the open door.

'Should I put on a lab coat?' she asked. 'Some people feel comforted by lab coats.'

He laughed, and reminded himself that he liked her, genuinely liked her.

'Sorry,' he said, and meant it. 'Just tense.'

'Worried?' she asked.

'No. Yes. A little. Tense.'

The room beyond was sparse, and reminded Hector a little of cop shows, and a little of old black and white sitcoms. *The ones where no room really looked lived in, worked in.* Blank walls, a small table by the door, and two large, slightly reclined leather-or-equivalent chairs. Walls in grey, chairs in brown, lighted squares in the ceiling. At least it was warm light.

The woman in the sweatshirt led them to the chairs, so like dentist chairs that, combined with the waiting room chairs, Hector thought it might all be on purpose. They laid back. Eve released his hand.

He repeated to himself that this was safe. *No butterflies, no flowers, no earthquakes across the globe.* They'd stressed that to him.

The woman in the sweatshirt had explained it all, very carefully, in another office not much farther down the hallway. That had been a month ago. She tried hard not to beat Hector over the head with maths that only the two women understood.

Sum over histories. The expanding wavefronts of our minds, the *two-slit* experiment. Waves and slits. His head had filled with scenes of storms at sea, layers of paint that you don't scrape off if you don't understand them. You just paint over.

Eve knew the score. She was the wrong kind of physicist, but she was a physicist. Hector had needed a drawing on a whiteboard. Like a child.

The photon takes many paths. Point A to point B is not just a straight line. It's *every* line, some not even straight. Infinite paths from A to B, and the photon takes them all. The world just *smooths things out,* the woman said. Each path has a probability. In the end, the photon seems to have taken only one path. But it really did take them all.

The whiteboard had looked like an exploding dandelion when she was done. Hector had nodded. The world is a dandelion.

Two others, in lab coats, wheeled the device into the room. It was small – remarkably small. It could have fit inside Hector's favourite camera bag. The cart came to rest between their chairs. Small electrode pads were applied to their temples. Blindfolds were placed over their foreheads, not pulled down over their eyes. Not yet.

Consciousness takes many paths. From point A to point B are a great many *decisions.* Some not straight. Infinite decisions, infinite paths, between one moment in life and another. Our minds – our *selves* – take every path. And then the world *smooths things out.* One decision, among the multitude, becomes *the* decision.

But we really did make them all. All the decisions.

Dandelions. Exploding dandelions of consciousness.

The woman was now standing between them, saying soothing things. It won't hurt. There would be a *merging,* she said.

Quantum particles aren't particles. Particle talk is handy, she said, but they aren't "things" – the woman had used her fingers to make the quotes. Quantum particles are *areas. Fields, at best.* But they don't exist *in one particular place.*

Or at one particular time.

Eternal exploding dandelions.

The woman looked down at them, there in their chairs. Electrodes adhered, innocuous brown box humming on the cart between them, almost inaudible.

'When you get there,' she said, 'you'll *be you.* That consciousness, in that moment, is *your consciousness.* It's *you.* You'll know that. There won't be two people there – just one. One Hector. One Eve.'

Eve smiled, and Hector didn't think anyone else could see the tension she shared with him.

'And then we just…' Eve said.

'You're just changing probabilities,' the woman said calmly.

'Okay,' Eve said.

'Okay,' Hector echoed, believably.

The machine hummed another, higher note.

There was a blurring. Not a blurring, Hector decided. More of a *fade,* like in the movies, when the director is taking you from one scene to the next. Only if the director stopped in the middle of the fade. The office is still there – the woman in the sweatshirt is still standing over you. Eve is still to your right. But the reception is there now too. Is there again. Is *still* there.

I'm seeing an office from my future, Hector thinks to himself, as he stands near the bar next to the dance floor. Then, *no. It's the office in the present. Just like this wedding is in the present.*

Hector remembered the reception. He remembered that night. He remembered the office, and the woman. The office of *now*. The reception of *now*.

What's the opposite of remembering, he asked himself. *For remembering what happens in the future*? *Premembering*? But that also was wrong. He heard the woman in the sweatshirt, saw her commingled with the dancing guests in front of him.

'Pull down the blindfold,' she said.

He did, and the office disappeared.

Hector looked, knew where Eve would be, even as he was looking for her. They met somewhere in the middle, bodies of the past and present swirling around them.

'So… this is… different,' she said. Then she laughed. Hector remembered, premembered how he loved that laugh.

'Right,' he said. 'It's funny how it isn't funny.'

She looked at him then, a surprised look on her face.

'I was just thinking… just now. Remember that we have to go look at that new car tomorrow.'

He nodded. 'We do. It looked good in the photos, guy says it runs okay. If it does, it's a good price. We should buy it.' He paused. 'We put, what, eighty thousand miles on that thing?'

'A hundred,' she said.

'A hundred,' he agreed. 'The second transmission.'

She looked around the room, at the clock. At the wedding party, still gathered at their table.

'Why don't we go somewhere. Talk. We still have time.'

Hector nodded. Why don't they talk? Why didn't they talk?

They made their way outside, off the stone patio where a few other guests would still have been able to hear them. The grass and turf gave way beneath their feet. *Flexibility*, Hector thought. Grass was so forgiving. They stopped at a low stone bench, down near the water. An unforgiving bench. They sat.

'Okay,' Eve started, like she started one of her classes, that same tone. 'We know, now. Both of us.'

'Yeah.'

Hector nodded. Years of knowing what he'd begin to learn a month from now hadn't come flooding all back, like a repressed memory – prememory. He'd known it all along, hadn't ever forgotten. There was nothing to remember. Nothing to learn. Nothing he didn't know.

'I remember this song,' he said, tilting his head back towards the hall. 'Haven't heard it in years. Since tonight, I don't think.'

'We sang along with it in the car, just yesterday, on the way. Then they played it here.' She scratched her head. 'Wasn't popular long.'

Out across the lake, somewhere in the trees, an owl called out. *Who-cooks-for-you? Who-cooks-for-you-aaaalllll?*

'I didn't think it would be this nice out,' he said. 'I didn't come out here all night. Forecast was rain, this morning.'

She was motionless, in the dark. 'I was out on the patio, for a while. Colder in a dress.' He could hear the smile in her voice. He reached out, took her hand, rested both his and hers on the bench between them.

'It's strange,' he said after a while. 'It's like when you're upset when a character in a movie dies. Isn't it?'

She laughed. 'It is. I know I'm upset. But I know its… it's not *fake*. It's…'

'Like waking up still angry from a dream,' he said.

'Like waking up,' she agreed.

The owl called again. Then a third time. No one responded to tell it who was in the kitchen.

'Not *upset*,' she said. 'I'm not upset. I'm *angry*.' She squeezed his hand. 'But... not now. You know. I *was*.'

'I know.' He looked for the owl, was never going to see it. 'I'm not upset. I'm sad. Lonely. But... you know.' He didn't say "not now".

The song changed again, behind them. A classic rock staple of classic weddings, a song Hector knew neither of them liked, neither of them had ever come to like.

'I'm so glad we're doing this,' she said very suddenly, with a release of a breath he hadn't known she was holding in. 'So, so glad.'

'Me too,' he smiled in the dark. And if he wasn't, he knew he would be. But he thought he really was.

She laughed again. 'Smoother is better. We've been all fractals since tonight. And... *god*, I *hate* this song.'

He stood then, in an exaggerated leap, and sang the next two lines along with the band. He reached his hands for the heavens, like any good music video would have him do.

She mimed gagging into the grass.

'Don't make me rethink the plan, bucko.' She let the song finish out, both of them looking off into the night.

'Okay,' she said, 'let's go be smooth.'

They walked back up the lawn, onto and across the patio. He wanted to take her hand again, but didn't bring himself to do it. They paused just inside the doorway, the music and dancing in full swing now.

'I feel bad,' he said. 'Ashamed.'

She nodded, swallowed. 'Even though.'

'Even though.'

'Do you think we'll feel bad… when it's changed?'

He considered. 'No idea. I'm just a brush-pusher. You're the physicist.'

They stood, watching the dancing.

'We'll feel *better*,' she said. 'Can't help but feel better.'

'Yeah. Okay… you ready?'

She nodded, and without a word slipped away from his side. She headed for the wedding party's table, where a few of the groomsmen were still sitting, laughing and drinking.

He set his shoulders and crossed the dance floor, pausing only for a chain of small children weaving their way through the adults, a mini conga line. He arrived at the bar, ordered the drink he knew he'd order, and leaned. He didn't have long to wait.

'Hector!'

He turned, smelling her perfume as she eased into the empty spot at the bar next to him. He smiled.

'I'm taking off,' the woman said. 'It was *great* to see you again… all these years.'

'Yeah,' he said, forcing a smile he remembered not having to force. 'Glad we could catch up.'

She pulled up her purse, dug inside, placed a couple of bills on the bar and slid them the bartender's way. The man nodded his thanks.

'And it was great to meet…'

'Eve,' he supplied.

'Right, Eve, sorry. It was great to meet her too.' Everything was great.

The bartender handed Hector his drink, and he raised it in a small toast to her instead of answering. She looked at him for a long second.

'Look,' she said. 'I've got a studio, back east. A bit small, but it's what we always talked about, back in school.'

He forced the same smile. 'Good for you! I'm working out of my garage. It's okay.' He didn't think she heard him.

'Like I said... you should come out and see it, sometime. I'll give you the grand tour. It's just a couple blocks from my apartment.' Her smile was effortful too, for different reasons.

Her hand dipped back into her purse, felt around, emerged with a business card between two fingers. She held it out to him.

Hector thought it would be harder. Like there would be a wall to push through, forces of the universe to contend with. A different Hector he'd have to fight. But it was easy. Like any other time he said no.

'No... no. I'm good here. I'm happy. Or... I will be. Sorry.' He really meant it, but knew it didn't need to be explained. Or couldn't be explained. And yet mixed signals were mixed signals. 'Sorry,' he said again. Meant it again.

She looked at him, away, and back. The business card hung for a moment, a shaking leaf, then went back into her purse.

'Okay. Yeah. Okay,' she said, and nodded like she understood what had happened. 'Well, take care.' And she meant it too. She pushed off from the bar, they exchanged smiles again. She headed for the parking lot.

Hector sighed, a mixture of relief and the mildest of regrets. The light was flashing through another slit, he hoped. The dandelion was exploding. *Mixed signals.* He looked across the room, found the head table.

198

Eve was leaning on the table, but one foot was already turned away from the discussion. On the other side, the groomsman was standing now. He sensed she was leaving, sensed his time was running out. Hector knew Eve was waiting for a moment, just as he had. What was it?

The groomsman reached into his coat pocket, pulled out his phone. He tapped it, slid a finger across the surface, tapped it again. He held it out to Eve then, with a nod down towards the screen. Hector could see the keyboard was visible.

That's the moment, he thought. '*Here, type your number in.*'

Hector smiled as Eve shook her head, said something brief. She held up her hand and then she was gone. Down off the step, away from the disappointed groomsman, onto the dance floor, and across the room. She caught Hector's eye when she was a few feet away. She smiled, shivered, nodded.

Done. Done and done.

Soon Eve was next to him again, there at the bar. He turned to her, about the say something, and stopped. The train of thought had entirely abandoned him. What was he going to say?

Something about the rest of the night? They would spend another hour here, neither of them enthusiastic about it. Then the drive home, uneventful. Easy?

Not easy.

Something about the next year? Some arguments, some fights. Nothing, he premembered, that couldn't be unsaid. Some counselling. He had thought that might be different. Still no children – that was interesting.

He sifted through his memories, both those of the past and those of the future. The list of the missing grew long. Lawyers, paperwork. Pills, lost friendships. Nope. None. Nowhere to be found.

He looked at her, found her already looking at him.

'Smoother,' she said, and her expression was fathoms deep. 'Smoother.'

He can see her – next to him in the office, in the fake leather chair. A few more lines on her face. A grey hair here or there – he knew she was still deciding on whether to cover those up. A little thinner, the Eve there in the office. The Eve with the ring on her finger.

She, he supposed, could see the same. She reached out for his hand, and he let her take it.

It would be smoother.

But then he could see another Eve. The Eve before him, and the Eve premembered in the office. But now another. Other memories – prememories – that he'd now had all along. Suddenly there the whole time.

Not three Hectors. Only one. Not four. Only one. Not…

He could see Eve before him, there in her blue dress, a far away look on her face now. Eve reclined in the chair in the office, blindfold over her eyes, lines on her face. Eve with more grey hair than brown now, reading in a chair, on the other side of the living room. A twenty-foot space a hundred feet across, floor lamp deepening her reading frown. Eve with even shorter hair, still grey, her image on his screen, foreign city lights behind her. She waves, ring on her finger. He waves back, the screen goes dark. Waves without smiles are not really waves, he decides. Decided.

Eve at the wedding looks at Hector at the wedding. She's no longer smiling now, either.

'Remember that studio?,' she asks. 'The one by the ware-house that we got you for your fiftieth birthday?'

'So I didn't have to work in the garage,' Hector remembers. Premembers. It was years after the cold office and fake leather chairs. He remembers the studio, filled with his paintings, rows and stacks of them. The products of late night after late night. The tones sombre, the brush strokes quick and aggressive. Not the paintings of his youth. But a host of them. When the shows and museums called, he always had paintings to send them. When they came to get them, late into the night, he was always there waiting.

He remembers her promotion, the one she didn't look for but grabbed at when it came. The one that would mean long days, weeks, away from home. He remembers that they both thought it was a good idea – both of them, bald Hector and grey-haired Eve. He would be fine, he said. She would be fine, she said.

Still no children, he remembers.

'I missed you,' he said, there at the bar. 'Until I didn't.'

'Right,' she said. 'I could have called more. But then I didn't.'

'Right,' he said.

He remembers his studio, filled with paintings. The couch, with blankets and pillow pushed to one end. Microwave, fridge, and a coffee pot standing by the sink. A mug with a toothbrush.

He remembers the ring, still on his finger. Still on his finger there at the wedding. There in the chair in the office. And still on his finger there in their home, as they recline in their own chairs now, side by side. A smaller brown box sits on a table between them – a table they would buy thirty years after the wedding. Fifteen-some years after that day in the office. The box looks mostly the same. The electrodes are smaller.

There is more, of course. Another house, her hair less grey, his less gone. His briefcase slumps against an easy chair, too-tight shoes discarded nearby. He watches her in the kitchen, on the phone, railing at a manager unseen and unsympathetic. They are both, he suspects, in that very moment thinking about the box again. The dandelions.

Then an apartment with a view of a city skyline, and then a ranch home in a suburb. All at once, but none together. A townhome in an old neighbourhood, ivy and broken sidewalks. Each one is smooth, painless. But each one is already faded before it has ended. Missed calls and half-empty closets, Chinese or Italian takeout and eating from the cartons.

She is still holding his hand, there at the wedding. Neither has spoken for a dozen lifetimes since the last song started. But they both understand, and are understood.

She squeezes, he squeezes back.

'It was smooth,' she said.

'Yeah. It *was* that. Every time.'

'We tried. Right?'

He squeezed harder. 'I *know* you did. I did too.'

'I know.'

They locked eyes, then released hands. The song changed again, another briefly popular song began.

'We sang this one too,' she said. 'In the car. In just a few minutes.'

'We did.' There was nothing to say now, nothing they hadn't said years from now.

'Good luck.'

She slipped away, back towards the head table. The grooms-man's head turned in her direction, and he smiled. Hector moved away from the bar, towards the doors, towards the parking lot, and towards the business card.

They had sung this song, he knew now. They'd sung them all.

THE TURNPIKE

Andrew Eastwick

Hernando leaned against the pump, gazing at the head-lights drifting along the Turnpike. The road was elevated, with a background of dark trees, and on the near side the hill sloped from the guardrail down to the brightly lit blacktop of the gas station. No one had stopped in a while, and Hernando chewed gum to pass the time and stay awake.

Then a pair of lights slowed and peeled off the pike on to the exit ramp, curling around the cloverleaf and pulling into the station. Hernando stayed put for as long as he could, then pushed off the pump with his shoulder blades, hands still buried in the pockets of his coveralls, and strolled toward the car as it rolled to a stop by the nearest pump.

The driver's door opened, and Hernando made an irritated sound in the back of his throat. Must be an out-of-stater. 'Hey, I got this,' he called.

But the driver didn't try to lift the nozzle or insert his credit card. He didn't even turn toward the pump. He just stood there for a moment with the door open, then staggered toward Hernando, who stopped in alarm. The man stopped, too, looked at Hernando, and fell dead at his feet.

Hernando crouched and took the man's pulse. There was none. He turned him over and checked for breathing. Nothing. He looked around. The car was dinging patiently because the door was open with the key still in the ignition. Hernando closed the door and crossed his arms on the roof of the car, looking at the oblivious headlights passing up there on the pike.

'Yo,' he said as he stepped into the garage.

'Yo,' came Tyrell's voice in reply, from beneath the car he was working on. Hernando said nothing else, and after a few moments Tyrell said, 'What's up?'

'Got a croaker.'

Tyrell was silent. The clanging of whatever he was doing to the undercarriage of the car stopped. Then he rolled out on his dolly and looked up at Hernando, his face smeared with grease.

'For real?' Tyrell asked.

'For real.'

Tyrell thought for a moment. 'First one in three years,' he said.

'Help me with him?'

They went out to where the driver lay dead, a few feet from his car.

'No shit,' Tyrell said.

Hernando took the legs and Tyrell took the arms and they carried him behind the station to the field of rusting and burned-out bodyshells and old tires and scraps even Tyrell didn't know what to do with. They took turns digging. When the hole was deep enough they laid the driver down in it and covered him up. While Hernando leaned on the shovel, wiping his brow with his sleeve, Tyrell crouched and pushed a hubcap into the dirt at the head of the grave.

'Well,' Tyrell said, joints cracking as he rose, 'I'm gonna get back.'

'I'm gonna go,' said Hernando.

Tyrell blinked at him. He looked away, to the Turnpike, then back at Hernando.

'Yeah?' he asked.

'Yeah.'

Tyrell blinked again. Then he stuck out his hand, and Hernando clasped it.

Tyrell went into the garage. Hernando heard his dolly roll back under the car and the tools clanging against the undercarriage. He went to the dead driver's car, got in and started it up. A commercial blared out of the radio. Then he pulled out of the station on to the access road, up the entrance ramp and on to the Turnpike.

He kept his speed reasonable and stuck to the middle and right lanes, passing only when he came up on someone going unusually slow. He surfed the radio, seeking music, but every station played commercials until he found a traffic report. That could be useful. Traffic was light going southbound with some congestion northbound. He realised he didn't know which direction he was going. He expected the traffic report to go back to other news, but the announcer kept talking about traffic, and Hernando stopped paying attention, letting the voice drift into the background of his driving. He watched the exit signs tick by as the voice droned on, and he was no longer sure if the report was still about the traffic on the Turnpike or on different roads.

His stomach rumbled. He couldn't remember when or what he had last eaten. Probably that package of Tastykakes back at the station. Before too long he saw a sign that said FOOD. He took the exit.

There was a diner, brightly lit amid the surrounding darkness, so he pulled into the parking lot and went inside. Sinatra was on the jukebox. No one was at the front counter. To his right stretched a long row of booths, empty save for an old man eating soup in the last booth, his fedora hanging on a hook. Hernando took a menu from the counter and sat down in the third booth.

He spread the menu on the Formica tabletop and flipped through the pages. It was longer than a car manual. He had accumulated twelve options and was beginning to narrow them down when a voice startled him:

'Hey hon, 't can I getcha?'

He looked up. The waitress wore a mustard-yellow uniform with more stains than his coveralls and an equally stained white apron. Her hair was teased up a foot above her head, with a little white cap perched precariously on top. She chewed gum and he realised he was still chewing gum, too. The skewed nametag on her chest said WANDA.

'Need another minute?'

'What's good here?' he asked, trying to remember the twelve options he had come up with.

'Most popular's the burger.'

'You like the burger?'

'My favourite's the club.'

'I'll have the club,' he said, shutting the menu with a thunk.

'Something to drink?'

He thought for a moment and decided he'd better have some coffee if he was going to keep driving.

'Coffee?' she prompted.

'Coffee.'

She wrote his order on her little pad, smiled, and walked away. Sinatra was still singing, but Hernando wasn't sure if it was the same song or a new one. He searched for a coin slot on the little jukebox flanked by salt and pepper shakers, but he couldn't find one. The buttons to change the display of song titles didn't work, and the titles themselves were obscured by the cloudy plastic covering. The old man from the end of the row walked past, tipped his hat, and went out. Hernando heard the rumble of the old man's car starting. The headlights flashed through the window, then tracked away as the old man backed out of the parking space and pulled out of the lot, toward the Turnpike.

The sound of the car faded and all that was left inside the diner was Sinatra's voice. This must be the third or fourth song, Hernando thought, but he hadn't noticed when it changed. It could have been the same song playing on repeat, or maybe he'd only been there a few minutes. He wasn't sure. He'd have to pay attention and listen for the gap between songs. But then he heard Wanda picking up the dishes and coins from the old man's table. He turned his head to look at her and she smiled and went through the swinging doors to the kitchen. Then it was quiet again except for Sinatra, and Hernando wondered if the song had changed while he'd been distracted by Wanda.

This time he really concentrated on the melody and lyrics, and he followed the song all the way to the bridge. Surely there would just be another verse and chorus and then he would catch it when the song switched, but then Wanda was back with his coffee.

'Here you go, Hernando,' she smiled.

He wondered how she knew his name, and then he looked down at his coveralls and saw it stitched there on his chest.

'Thanks, Wanda.'

'Food'll be right out,' she said, and disappeared again. He heard part of a verse and a chorus but now he couldn't remember what he had just been listening to and wasn't sure if it was the same song or a new one. It went into a new verse as he sipped his coffee, and he gave up. Then Wanda was sliding a plate in front of him, with a club sandwich cut into quarters. Each quarter was as tall as his hand was long and was held together with a toothpick.

'Enjoy,' she smiled, and started to walk away, but he asked if she was hungry. She stopped. 'Yeah,' she said, 'I guess.'

'You said you like the club?'

'Yeah.'

'Have mine,' he said, pushing the plate across the table, 'and order another one for me.'

'It's so big. I can only eat half.'

'I can only eat half, too. Let's share.'

They put the plate in the middle. Wanda pulled out her gum and stuck it on the rim of the plate. Hernando did the same. She took her quarters of the sandwich apart and ate the bacon first. He broke his down into eighths.

'This is good,' he said.

'Mm-hmm.'

They chewed in silence for a few moments.

'This jukebox,' he said, 'does it only play Sinatra songs? Or is it the same song on repeat? Or just one long song that never ends?'

'I don't know.'

He tapped a fingertip against a corner of his own mouth. Her tongue flicked out.

'Other side,' he said.

She flicked her tongue out the other side and licked a glob of mayo. She laughed, and he laughed too.

'You never noticed?' he asked.

'The mayo?'

'The jukebox.'

She shook her head.

'I've been trying to– '

She pressed a finger to her lips, and he thought she was telling him he had food on his mouth, but then he realised she was telling him to be quiet. They both listened intently to the jukebox. A car pulled into a parking space and cut the headlights and the engine. Wanda got up from the booth and went to the front, exchanged a few words with the customer who came in, and then went to the kitchen. She came back out with a bag and handed it to the customer. The cash register dinged.

She returned to the booth. In the meantime Hernando had finished his half of the sandwich and the cup of coffee and had failed to notice if the song had changed.

'I'm finished with this,' Wanda said, waving at the deconstructed bits of sandwich on her plate. 'You want it to go?'

He shook his head. 'How much I owe you?'

'On the house,' she smiled.

'Thanks,' he smiled, and stood up.

'So they let you leave.'

'Huh?'

'You work at a gas station, don't you?'

He nodded.

'And they let you go?'

'I just left,' he shrugged.

She stared at him, incredulous.

'You ever leave this place?'

She shook her head and asked, 'Where'd you go?'

'Here. I came here.'

'That's all?'

'So far.'

'So what do you do, out there? Just drive?'

'Yeah. Isn't that what people do?'

'I don't know. No one's ever talked to me about it.'

'Me neither.'

She looked out the window. He followed her gaze to the passing headlights.

'Come with me,' he said.

Her eyes flashed. She glanced at the doors to the kitchen, then back at him. 'Really?' she asked.

'Really.'

'Where are you going?'

'Out on the Turnpike.'

'What will you do when you get to the end?'

'There's an end?'

'Well yeah, I mean, there has to be, right?'

He thought for a moment. 'Turn around and go back the other way, I guess,' he said.

'Could you get off and not go back?'

'I don't know.'

She looked back at the kitchen again. Her eyes were wide and the corners of her mouth twitched but her easy smile didn't come. She looked out the window, then at him.

'Okay,' she said, breaking into a grin.

He reached for his gum, stuck to the rim of the plate, but she pulled out a pack and handed him a fresh stick. She took a stick too and they chewed as they walked out.

Hernando headed for the driver's side but stopped.

'You know how to drive?' he asked.

'I think so,' she said. 'Yeah. I remember.'

'You drive.'

They passed in front of the car to switch sides. He handed her the keys and their fingers touched, lingering for a moment before sliding apart. He got in the passenger's side and she got in the driver's side and turned the key. The traffic report was still on the radio. Wanda changed the station and a saxophone solo burst from the speakers.

They looked at each other and smiled, and she pulled out of the diner lot and on to the Turnpike to join the other cars drifting through the night.

THE AUTHORS

CORMACK BALDWIN is a speculative fiction author and editor who once made a blood pact with a god (he's fine). His works have appeared in anthologies, podcasts, and magazines, as well as cafes, parks, and thrift stores. He is the head archivist (Editor-in-Chief) of *Archive of the Odd*, a speculative found-fiction magazine. You can find a list of his works at **cmbaldwin.carrd.co**, or the man himself **@cormackbaldwin** on Twitter.

DIE BOOTH is a queer indie author who likes wild beaches and exploring dark places. When not writing, he DJs at *Last Rites* – the best (and only) goth club in Chester, UK. You can read his prize-winning stories in anthologies from Egaeus Press, Flame Tree Press and many others. His books, including his cursed new novella *Cool S* are available online. You can find out more about his writing at **diebooth.wordpress.com** or say hi on Twitter **@diebooth.**

DANNY BRENNAN is a writer, organiser & collaborative artist working across disciplines. His work seeks to build new worlds inside the shell of the old.

ARIA K. C. is an Irish writer based in Galway City, primarily interested in experimental approaches to fiction. A trans woman, Aria also focuses on themes of dysphoria and gender within her work. She recently completed the first draft of her first novel, a tale set in her hometown which she describes as, *"An emotional, lyrical and contemporary Irish take on magic-realism."* Occasionally Aria dabbles in filmmaking and music.

BRIANNA CUNLIFFE is an environmental justice advocate and storyteller. In 2019, she served as the artist-in-residence on the Kent Island Scientific Station in the Bay of Fundy, generating poetry, short stories, and essays focused on the climate crisis. Her work has been published in *Reckoning Magazine, Lucent Dreaming, Storm Cellar, Claw and Blossom, Isacoustics*, Blind Corner,* and more. She is deeply committed to using the power and joy of story to help us imagine more just futures for our ecosystems and for all of us.

JAMES DWYER lives in Midleton, Ireland, and works as a writer by day and a martial arts instructor by night. He has published short stories in anthologies with Beagle North and Anansi Archive, and fantasy novels with Indie Publishing, Paused Books. When not enjoying time with his wife and kids, James loves nothing more than to read, write, and fight.

ANDREW EASTWICK was born and raised in New Jersey and lives in Los Angeles with his wife, actor/improviser Tara Copeland, their daughter Maggie and cat Ozmo. He is the Senior Grant Writer for After-School All-Stars, a national nonprofit organization that provides enrichment programs for underserved youth.

CHRIS FITZPATRICK has published short stories and poetry in the past and is a regular contributor to newspapers. His first collection of poetry, *Poetic Licence in a Time of Corona*, was published in May 2022 by Twenty First Centruy Renaissance. He has also written for the stage.

JENNIFER HUDAK is a speculative fiction writer fueled mostly by tea. Her work has appeared on both the *Locus Magazine* and the *SFWA* recommended reading lists, and has been twice nominated for a Pushcart Prize. Originally from Boston, she now lives with her family in Upstate New York where she teaches yoga, knits pocket-sized animals, and misses the ocean. Find out more about her at **JenniferHudakWrites.com**.

TOM JAVOROSKI is a writer of speculation and teacher of philosophy, a cyclist and a gamer and many other things to varying degrees of volume and skill. He has been published at *Every Day Fiction*, and has credits in a handful of RPG books. He's in the Midwest, surrounded by gravel roads, unless he's Hulder hunting in Norway. And he's thrilled beyond measure that you're reading this.

ARAN KELLY has recently finished a Creative Writing Masters at UCC.

LARK MORGAN LU lives with a collection of succulents and tea. They have been previously published in *Augur Magazine*. Find them at **LarkMorganLu.com.**

JAMIE PERRAULT is a queer agender veterinarian living and working in the American Midwest. When not reading or writing, they can be found hiking, playing the clarinet, or watching tokusatsu shows. They have a wonderful spouse, and twin five-year-olds. They have had work published in *Apparition Literature*, the *Crow's Quill* online literary horror magazine, and several independent anthologies. They can be found online at **jamieperrault.com** or on Twitter **@awritinghope**.

COURTNEY SMYTH is from Dublin. They are a writer of both short and long stories about people, places and things. They have previously been published in *Paper Lanterns Literary Journal* and *The Last Five Minutes of a Storm* anthology. Their debut novel, *The Undetectables*, will be published in 2023.

DAVID D. WEST lives and writes in the Pacific Northwest. The gloomy atmosphere of the region's rainy forests and grey beaches provides the perfect setting for his writing.

Printed in Great Britain
by Amazon

23148027R10126